D0559413

The Golden Acre

Thyra Ferré Bjorn

2/21

The Golden Acre

FLEMING H. REVELL COMPANY

Old Tappan, New Jersey

Library of Congress Cataloging in Publication Data

Bjorn, Thyra Ferré.
    The Golden Acre.

    I.   Title.
PZ4.B626Go   [PS3552.J6]   813'.5'4   74-23893
ISBN 0-8007-0691-9

TO
Dr. Robert Ernst
and
in memory of Dr. Matthew Bachulus

The Golden Acre

1

She was the last patient of the day. Dr. Ernest Omar heaved a sigh of relief as he stared at the closed door. He could hear Mrs. Dixon's clicking heels as she walked down the hall.

Poor soul, he was thinking. She was one of the brave ones, and yet it had been hard to tell her the truth—that an operation was needed immediately, that her breast would have to be removed. The lump was large now and she, like so many others, had waited too long to see a doctor. He feared for her, and her smile hurt him in a strange way, because her eyes were filled with tears that spilled down over her cheeks.

"I trust you," she had said in a soft voice, "and whatever will be . . . will be."

He had smiled back at her, encouragingly.

"You are young and strong, Mrs. Dixon. I assure you that I will do all in my power to help you. I just wish that you had come to me a year ago."

"I know—I felt it then, but it was such a little thing, and I didn't want it to be real. I tried to ignore it, to tell myself that it wasn't there or that it would go away. I'm sorry now, but I have a lot of confidence in you, so I'll try not to be afraid."

They set the date for the hospital, and soon he would know if she could be saved. But in his mind he feared the worst for her. A frown creased his strong brow and his mahogany-brown eyes saddened at these depressing thoughts.

There had been too much of this lately, he thought. Why did they have to wait until it was too late? Too many troubled souls seemed to seek his help, bracing themselves for the fact they could not escape, yet hoping that an operation would solve it all. Much later, many would return, knowing that they were facing the end. They would come in tears, searching for comfort, although they knew that life could not be extended, that he was a surgeon with but limited powers over life and death. Systematically, Dr. Omar marked Mrs. Dixon's card and placed it in the file under *D*.

Nancy Cook, his capable nurse, had gone an hour ago. Today had been a full day for both of them, but at least Nancy's working time had a reasonable limit. His seemed endless, and now there was this new case to worry about. But he must stop now and try to relax. Dr. Omar stretched his cramped, tired limbs and looked out the floor-length window onto the city below, now glowing with thousands of brilliant multicolored lights. He opened the side window wide to let the cold winter air flow into his office. The air made him feel alive, and he inhaled deeply. Yes, below lay the city—the busy city of Boston! How gay it looked from this height; the view at night was breathtakingly lovely.

How well it hid its true face, he brooded, wrapped in flickering neon, the gleaming splendor of light upon light, one more colorful than the next. Under this cover the city hid its crimes, tears, and frustrations. Each light represented a dwelling, be it home or apartment, a store, a business, or an amusement place. And the people mingling down there—how well he knew them. The rushing, pushing crowd was restless, aimlessly searching for something that forever eluded them—the old world that used to be, the safe, contented era of yesterday.

Once he had been a part of that bygone world—where a man's word had value and integrity, and honesty ruled in business as honor did in family living. But that world was gone forever; it rested among the dead in the cemeteries outside the city. And the peace and joy that he used to feel were gone, too. He seemed unable to lose himself in the great work to which his life was dedicated, no matter how much effort he exerted. Dr. Ernest Omar felt tired and old—old at forty-eight—and weary to his limits with the whole situation. He slumped in the chair by his desk and held his head in his hands, as demanding pressures stormed his brain.

I am not going to take it any longer, he told himself. I cannot bear the strains of today. There must be some place, one little acre somewhere, where I could find peace and rest.

The last ten years had seemed as long as a whole lifetime. Everything around him had changed, and dark shadows seemed to lurk everywhere. Even his church had changed. It had happened gradually, but now he found he could not relax even when he sat in a pew with his family on Sunday mornings. The church was the same historic one of his childhood, where he used to find peace. But now when he left the sanctuary, he carried the same burdens he had brought with him, and he found himself even more tense and deeply disappointed. If this was the House of God, He was strangely missing. Dr. Omar's hope for eternity seemed to grow dim. Perhaps there was nothing to it, after all. Religion seemed to be as polluted as the air he had to breathe, and pollution of the mind and soul seemed to have eroded even the Temple of God. And outside the church, the current teachings of free thought and free love seemed to him as deadly as the cancer he fought as a doctor.

Where would he find peace? Was there no place in the city that was safe? Even this towering, high-rent building which housed his office on the eleventh floor could easily be blown up one day by some fanatical group of youngsters who thought they were doing God and His world a favor. He knew that Barbara, his lovely wife, feared the city, too.

She was a busy woman—the house was large and she prided herself on her domestic skills. He was glad, too, that her compassion and energy had led her also to days filled with the activity of good works. She was among the first to be called upon for help with fund-raising activities, and he thought she enjoyed her hospital volunteer hours. Now that their daughter was almost adult (how frightening that was), Barbara had put more and more of her vitality into serving where needed in the church and community. But there was always so much just crying to be done, and he knew that the pace got a little frantic at times. In unguarded moments she revealed her growing concern about the frenzy of people, traffic, and responsibilities which seemed to push them both aimlessly along.

Dear Barbara—her still-slim figure moved a little slower lately, those blue eyes were less sparkling, and apparently the strain of their lives in bustling Boston had brought a few lines to her face as well as a tendency to twist a handkerchief nervously through her gentle fingers. She even seemed reluctant to face the driving and parking problems now associated with attending the concerts and plays they had once found so enjoyable.

For a long time now when he kissed her good-bye in the morning, Barbara would cling to him for a moment, looking up at him with anxious eyes and say, "Have a good day, Ern . . . and a safe one."

"Sure thing, Hon. I'll be back at dinner time. Come on now, I'm perfectly safe. Don't worry!"

But as he drove from their home in Lexington into Boston each morning, he wondered if his words rang true. As a doctor there *were* things to worry about. Besides the misguided fanatics, there were the dope addicts who would stop at nothing to get into the locked drug cabinets in his office, or at least into his black bag. Those poor devils, driven by their burning hell, would give or do anything just to get a fix, no matter how temporary.

No, Barbara was right. Nothing was safe in the city and the pollution grew worse daily and the traffic was becoming more dangerously entangled. What was the solution for it all?

Tomorrow he had two operations to perform. Only God knew how much he wanted them to be successful. And although his religion seemed diluted, he knew his heart called out to God for help many times when the scalpel was placed in his hand and he began to cut into the diseased flesh. To be a cancer specialist these days was an awesome task. And such a doctor could not even relax and write off his case after the operation. Sometimes it took years before he was sure of the outcome.

So, why then did he continue this madness? He could take action and be a free man. Oh, for that old feeling of security—to laugh and play and enjoy the good side of life. He did not want this just for himself, but even more for the two persons who meant more to him than any others in the whole world—his wife, Barbara, and his daughter, Gail.

Gail would be eighteen this June, when she would graduate from high school. This kind of life was not for her. He and Barbara must shield her from this evil world, or at least take her away from the danger zone.

He must find that peaceful acre, perhaps in New Hampshire among the White Mountains or in Maine or Vermont. There must be a place somewhere like the one that now existed only in his mind. Tonight he would have a long talk with Barb and together they would reach the only sensible decision—he could sell his practice, or if it proved to be too difficult to sell, he would ask one of the young surgeons who often assisted him to take over for a couple of years. In that way he could start his retreat. As soon as he had decided definitely, he would not schedule any more surgery. He would notify his patients of the day he was leaving and the name of his replacement.

As Dr. Omar drove home toward Lexington that night, his heart felt light, and he noticed once more the beauty in the snowflakes that covered the branches of the spreading trees. He knew now that he was on the right track, that the idea had been imbedded in his subconscious for a long, long time. It was he who had kept it from coming to the surface. Now if only Barbara would agree, all would be right.

The Omars always ate dinner by candlelight. It was restful, provided a cozy atmosphere, and seemed right in the old house in which they lived. Barbara Omar was an expert in bringing forth the beauty from everything she touched, and she never minded the extra work. She was an excellent cook and the dishes she served often resembled magazine displays. He was a lucky man to have such a wife. On cold nights there was always a fire in the dining-room fireplace. The old house had six fireplaces and most of them were kept in use during the winter months.

Tonight a fire blazed in the dining room as he had anticipated and dinner was waiting as both Barbara and Gail greeted him in the foyer.

"My goodness, Dad, was I glad when I heard you stamping the snow off your feet. You're so late tonight that Mom and I were hoping you hadn't had an accident. It must be slippery."

"No, driving isn't really that bad and our world looks beautiful with this new snow. I had a late appointment at the office. They seem to run later and later every week, and tomorrow morning I have two operations, so I have to leave the house early."

"Did you have to schedule two in one morning?" asked Barbara.

"In both cases, yes. I'm afraid they are both too far gone already. But let's forget the doctor part of me for tonight. It's so good to be home."

He gave each of them a light kiss and led the way into the dining room. The warming flames felt good, and for the first time in months he seemed to relax as he sipped his tomato juice and nibbled on some crackers. As always, there was lively conversation around the dinner table.

Gail bubbled enthusiastically over some nice comments which the history teacher had scrawled on her latest term paper. She was in an exuberant mood, and even insisted on demonstrating, between courses, the latest school cheer, sobering suddenly as she remembered to tell her parents about the Jackson boy down the street, who had been picked up by the police the night before, on a drugs charge.

At this point it was difficult for Dr. Omar not to dive into one of his lectures on the dangers lurking in today's world. He knew that Gail didn't need a lecture—she was a fine young woman who seemed fully convinced of the errors inherent in some of the new ways and thinking with which other young people were experimenting. Still . . . the doctor pushed his fears aside as he remembered that tonight he and Barbara would reach a decision which would provide sanctuary for them all.

He turned his attention back to their meal—the pork roast was almost too pretty to carve, he joked, so beautifully decorated with apricots, stuffed prunes, and parsley! This was the life he loved—a dear family which showed its love, good food, and the warmth of home.

After dinner, when Gail had gone to her room to finish her homework, he would mention his plans to Barbara. The fire threw a warm glow over the living room and Ernest Omar, relaxing in his favorite reclining chair, eyed the evening paper while Barbara finished a few chores in the kitchen. Soon she joined him, curling up on the davenport.

"And now, what is your important news, Ern?" she asked.

Omar looked at his wife in surprise.

"How did you know I had something important to talk about tonight?"

She smiled. "It's written all over your face, dear. You aren't very good at hiding your inner emotions from me."

"I didn't know it was that obvious, but I'm not surprised. My idea is so exciting that I could have shouted it all the way home from Boston."

"Then, out with it!"

"Barbara, I have decided to retire, to resign my position, close down my practice and move away from it all. Are you with me?"

"It depends upon where you are taking me! You are much too young to retire. Couldn't you go somewhere else to practice?"

"I don't know yet. Just now I'm fed up. I can't take it any longer. The city is draining my whole being, and I worry about Gail—the air she breathes, the danger she faces on the streets, the strange morals and drugs that are such a part of the city. I'd like to find a place where life is relaxed and easy, where we can live as a family without fear. Contentment is all I want, Barbara, and safety for my family. We have enough money to live if we choose a simple life. In fact, I don't even think Gail should go on to college. All she'd learn there is to be different."

"Of course she should go to college! It is not *that* bad, I hope."

"But it is, honey, and it's getting worse every year. Free love is replacing moral conduct and the students' thirst for learning seems to have been lost in the desire for new experiences and drugs. Gail is too pretty and innocent to be destroyed by all that."

"How do you think she will feel about it?"

"I don't know. I don't even plan to ask her. If we find a place, we will just move. Surely she can delay college for a year."

"But she has already been accepted at Skidmore."

"Well, that's not so hard to remedy. But it would be better not to tell her anything about it, for now. I bet she'll see it our way after a while. Just let our plan take its course. We'll take one day at a time—now when we can really begin living."

They talked long into the night and before they went to

sleep Barbara had agreed that they should look for a place in the mountains, and just let Gail's acceptance fall by the wayside. Was it really that important? She could always go to college another year, they reasoned. A year away from everything would do her good. She would mature and be better equipped to face the dangers and temptations of the world.

Barbara had hesitated, at one point. "Perhaps we should give it more time, Ern. Do we have to decide tonight?"

"Yes, we do. If I'm going to retire, I have to decide now. This is such a big decision, I can't bear toying with it. If I'm wrong, I will still be young enough to go back. But at least I would have had a year or two to get my old self back and begin to believe in life again."

"I guess you're right, Ern. This *is* important. If we're going to do it, we had better do it quickly; then it will be less painful."

Long after Barbara was asleep that night, Dr. Omar lay wide awake. There was so much to think about. His action would come as a shock to his patients. He must break the news to them gently. He would carry out his obligations and perform all scheduled surgery. But after this night he would book no more. He would put his practice in good hands. This should not take too long—there were many competent young doctors he knew who would be glad to take over his office. By June, just after Gail's graduation, they could be ready to move.

Now the old house in Lexington was still. The ashes in the hearth threw off a soft dusty glow. Outside, the snowstorm was over. It had been just a January storm in New England, and many other storms would blow over the area before spring arrived. Tonight, frost and ice might be reigning outside, but as Dr. Omar drifted off to sleep, his mind toyed with thoughts of coming summer, of mountains and waterfalls, of a low house far away from the noisy city with an acre of land surrounding it, and maybe even a brook or lake where he could fish. He was at ease now because Barbara had not objected, and as for Gail, she was still not strong enough to try her own wings. Before she did, he would clip them just enough so she could not fly very far from the new life that would soon be waiting in a rosy future.

What a dear sweet child she was. No generation gap in this house! Gratefully he remembered that Gail had always rewarded their devotion with a charming obedience that was becoming rare in the youth of today. Never had she given them cause for worry and he was confident that her good sense and respect for their wishes would not desert her, with this minor disappointment.

2

When spring arrived with its budding trees and green-
ing lawns, Dr. Omar's plans had begun to take shape.
After much deliberation he had decided not to sell his
practice, but rather to find a partner who could step right
into the office and take over, telling the patients only that
Dr. Omar was taking time off for rest. This solution
seemed wiser in the long run, more sensible than dropping out of the picture completely. Then, if being liber-
ated from all the responsibilities of medicine did not suit
him, he could make an easy return. Barbara had agreed
fully with this plan.

"This is the right thing to do, Ern. Keeping your name
on that door and adding another under yours will not
make the step you're taking seem so final. After all, it will
be a big change after having been a doctor for so many
years. But whose name will you add?"

"I have already chosen my partner," beamed Omar. "I
am really in luck! Dr. Haas has been looking for a partner-
ship. Herbert is a top-notch surgeon, careful and dedicated. For a long time I have admired his skill and calm

manner as we worked together in the operating room. That doctor is one who is headed for the top someday."

"Have you talked to him about it?"

"I have, and he's delighted, if we can work out the details. He's newly married and has been looking for an established doctor to join. Of course he had no idea that I was looking for a partner. If he is willing, I couldn't find a better man for my patients. I hope you can meet him soon."

"Well, that is easy enough! Invite Dr. Haas and his wife here for dinner. Any night next week is fine with me."

"That will be a wonderful way to get acquainted —perhaps one of the best. Thanks for the idea, Barb!"

So the Omars entertained the Haases, and Barbara was delighted with them both. The dinner seemed to be a great success. The groundwork was laid for communication.

The old Lexington house held both Herbert and Lois Haas spellbound.

"I don't see how you can leave it, Barbara," said Lois. "If I lived in a home like this, I don't think I would ever look for another place. Can't you retire and be happy here?"

Barbara smiled. "Not since Ernest began to dream about his Golden Acre, as he's begun to call our retreat. He wants land, brooks, lakes, and mountains, and most of all, to get away from people."

"Well, all I can say is that the family who buys this house will get more than just a house."

"How about renting it from us?" suggested Dr. Omar.

The room was deadly silent for a moment.

"Do you really mean that, Ernest? And another question—could we afford it?"

"Yes, I mean it! And since this furniture would not fit the place I have in mind, you can rent it furnished. And since I know you would take good care of everything, I would lease it to you at a price you could afford—with only one clause."

"And what would that be?"

"That we could have it back on two months' notice, if we so desired."

The Haases exchanged glances and again a brief stillness fell over the dining room. Soon Lois and Herb nodded eagerly and they all retired to the living room and began to discuss details and prices. When Dr. and Mrs. Haas left that night, everything was settled, both the practice and the house. By the first of July the new tenants would be moving into the Lexington house, and by that time the Omars would surely have found their Golden Acre.

After their guests had gone, Barbara and Ernest relaxed contentedly in the living room. It was as though a great burden had slipped from their shoulders.

"Everything seems to have fallen into place," smiled Barbara. "I just have a feeling that this is our destiny and that soon we will find what we are looking for. Then all our worries will be over."

After that night, the Omars spent every Wednesday and Sunday driving through New Hampshire and Vermont. They read real-estate ads and took their time looking, but finding the house that existed in their imaginations was no easy task, until late one Wednesday, they literally stumbled upon it.

Barbara had packed sandwiches, fruit, and a thermos of coffee in a wicker basket for the outing. Gail had been invited to a girl friend's home for dinner, so there was no rush to return to Massachusetts. After their picnic among tall pines, the Omars followed a narrow country road which seemed to disappear far ahead in the majestically rising White Mountains, when suddenly—there it stood, right in front of them!

The house was weathered and tumbledown, but it was built in the style of a country home of the comfortable past. There was at least an acre of cleared, though weed-overgrown, land around it, before the sturdy pines, crisp blue spruce, birch, and maple took over. A small brook bubbled through the backyard and also visible from the house was a small mountain lake with water as clear as glass. The house was seemingly in a no-man's-land, but there was a small sign on the back door reading: IF YOU ARE INTERESTED IN THIS GOD-FORSAKEN PLACE, IN-QUIRE AT THE WHITE HOUSE ON THE MOUNTAIN.

It did not take the Omars long to decide. They *knew* this was it, even before they had walked around the house several times and peered in all the windows. Tramping through the yard, they discovered an old wishing well overgrown with moss, its base sprinkled with delicate violets and sunny buttercups. The brook played a merry tune as it gurgled through the rear, gray water turning white as it foamed over the rocks—native granite, stable and sure. Birch, ash, and maple trees loomed protectively over the early-flowering dogwood and laurel, and from the stone crevices peeked hints of columbine reds and yellows to come. The city dwellers noted with delight that jack-in-the-pulpit and lily-of-the-valley plants stood bravely at the stream's edge. A rickety wooden bridge carried the Omars into a small orchard beyond.

"These must be apple or cherry or something," said the doctor. "I've just discovered that I know very little about trees."

"They could be pear or plum, for all I know," laughed Barbara. "You see, I'm as dumb as you about nature, but we'll both learn—because I love this old place already. The house is even the right color, though maybe it needs some fresh gold paint."

"I love it, too!" Ernest looked up at the towering mountains. "I'd like to announce to the whole world," he shouted in his booming bass voice, "that I have found my Golden Acre. Come on, hon, let's drive up that mountain road and see those people in the big white house; it must be at least a half a mile away."

The road up the mountain was steep, curving dangerously in places, but the Omars made it before the sun began to set in the west, turning the scene below into a lake of gold. Mr. and Mrs. Briggs, the people in the white house, were a friendly old couple.

"We're glad you are interested," Mr. Briggs said slowly, "but before you buy it, we'd like to know something about you. You see, this whole mountainside is ours. Other neighbors are miles away. We don't want anyone to buy the house on speculation. We feel it has to be used for the home it was once meant to be. The house has a sad story. Judy, our only daughter, was to be married and to have moved into the house as a young bride. It was new then, built for her by her husband-to-be. There was never a happier couple and they had worked so hard to make the house the dream they wanted it to be. We can still hear their laughter—we used to drive down there on summer nights to see how they were progressing. It was like a part of heaven—their special place."

The old man, who had been telling the story, stopped suddenly. He shook out his handkerchief, wiped a tear that had rolled down his cheek.

"You tell the rest, Mama," he said, turning to his gray-haired wife.

They were still standing beside the car on the driveway by the white house.

"Come and sit down on the porch, please." The old lady smiled faintly but her eyes were shadowed by sadness as though the task her husband had asked of her was more than she could bear. The Omars followed her up the steps and sat down in the wicker chairs on the screened porch overlooking a breathtaking view of the valley below.

"You've seen the road," she began, "how it curves and how steep it is. Even though it is less than half a mile down to the house in the valley, one must drive with the utmost care, and we all travel that way, knowing its dangers very well. The road has written its own law, engraved deep in our minds. It was always so, but Bernard and I have lived here over forty years, and we have no fear of the road, although we travel it only when we go down to shop or to church or for something special.

"Well, on the night before the wedding, the church had been decorated with laurel and wild flowers, and our daughter's home was ready. She and Tom were not even going on a honeymoon; they were just delighted to spend it in their new home. The time was so exciting for the young ones. They had come up here for dinner, and instead of Judy staying home, she wanted to go down just once more to her love nest, as she called it. We don't know how it happened! Perhaps she was so lovely that Tom couldn't take his eyes from her . . . but the car went out of control and it rolled down over the cliff. When help finally reached them . . . there was no life."

She stopped talking, her tearless eyes looking into the distance as though she scanned time and eternity.

"We were glad they went together. One could not have lived without the other. God took them . . . and we are left here childless and growing older, but so grateful that we still have each other."

Her husband spoke up then. "But that is not all. For some reason, I have a feeling you would be the right people to buy the property. We have only rented it before, furnished as it was before the wedding, though I suppose most of the furniture is old and shabby by now. For the last two years we have had no tenants because we feel obligated to tell them the story and of the curse."

"We call it a curse," interrupted his wife. "Something tragic has happened to each family who has rented the house. One man was thrown from his horse and broke his back . . . one lost a finger chopping firewood, and a little boy only two years old, drowned in the brook. That was the last one. Something is wrong with the house!"

"But we don't believe in such curses," said Dr. Omar. "Such things happen to families wherever they live, and the house can't be blamed. No, those things don't frighten us!"

"Fine! But we have warned you! Bernard, give them the key to the house. Take a look inside. Think over what we have said. Then come back and let us know."

"May we have until next Wednesday?"

"Sure, why not! Let us know a week from today what you have decided."

The Omars drove down the hill carefully; the story they had just heard was fresh in their minds. Barbara breathed a sigh of relief when they reached the valley again. There was still enough light to take a look at the rooms inside. With a strange feeling that the young couple's spirits hovered close to the house, the Omars felt almost as if they were treading on sacred ground. The house was beautifully laid out, with a big old-fashioned fireplace in the kitchen, which made them love the house even more. But darkness was falling over the mountains, and they had to start back. For some strange reason they both felt that this would be their future home. They were so sure! In a way, they felt as if they had just found shelter from the stress and conflict of modern living.

They discussed their feelings as they drove down the highway.

"There is something about that place, Barbara, that makes me feel as if I have already lived there. That's how at peace I feel."

"I have the same feeling, Ern. This must be our future home—and what possibilities it has! We can give away the old furniture and buy just the right thing for each room. What fun it will be to shop. We'll let Gail choose her own furniture; she'll love that. I wonder how she will like Golden Acre."

"She better not see it until we have fixed it up a little. I have the feeling, Barbara, that she won't be able to see the possibilities we do, especially in its present condition."

"Well, after next Wednesday we can go right to work. Perhaps we should do the outside first and then refinish the inside gradually. Do you realize that the Briggses gave us the key without even asking our names? I never knew such trust still existed."

That night they told Gail about the house, but not of its story or its curse. Gail did not seem too enthusiastic, but she listened and smiled and let them think that she was glad they had found just what they wanted.

The following Wednesday morning the sun was shining brightly as Barbara and Ernest started off just after

Gail had left for school. They could not wait to see the house again and there it stood, waiting for them as before, with the brook gurgling its music, the birds singing from the tall trees, and the air fresh and pure. They both gratefully filled their lungs with unpolluted air.

"Oh, Barbara," said Ernest, "to think there is still a spot like this left here on earth."

They walked hand in hand up to the lake where the water was so clear they could see to the bottom even though it was very deep. The day was one of discovery —for here they found peace, quiet, and tranquility—and for a while they were content to sit on the front steps, drinking in the beauty of their surroundings. Finally, they attended to the tricky business of driving up the steep hill to the big white house once again. Prices and papers had to be put in order, and there had to be a down payment to hold the property. The Briggses already seemed like old friends.

A couple of weeks later, Golden Acre would belong to the Omars, and they both counted the days until they could move, until Ernest would not have to leave each morning to minister to the sick, but could give all his time to this haven of quiet, turning it into one of the most beautiful spots this side of heaven.

Now the days in the office seemed longer than ever to Ernest. Turning patients away had not been easy, but Dr. Haas was taking over and he seemed to win people's confidence. Dr. Omar could not have found a finer doctor, and although he was grateful for Dr. Haas's instant popularity, a tiny stab of jealousy stung his heart. He had not expected his patients to take to a new doctor so quickly and wholeheartedly.

Soon he would forget all this. Yes, just as soon as he

could bid Boston good-bye and start out for his new world, hospitals, sickness, pain, and tears would be forgotten. Then he could leave the doctor part of him behind and become a new man—one who could enjoy life to its fullest. And with each day that passed, that time was growing nearer.

3

The heavy spring night was hung with a dense fog, but inside Dr. Omar's large living room a bright fire blazed in the fireplace, warming the three members of the family who sat in their comfortable chairs watching a television movie. At the end of the movie, the doctor crossed the room and abruptly snapped off the set.

"Why, Dad," said Gail with annoyance, "I wanted to see the next program. Why did you shut it off?"

"Because I want a little time to talk with my family. There are some things we need to discuss and tonight is as good a time as any, since we're all right here. I hope you don't mind missing the show, but what I want to say is pretty important."

"No, the TV doesn't really matter. But what's so serious that we all have to discuss it?"

"Our future plans, honey. And because you are deeply involved, I want everything out in the open."

Gail looked at her father. He seemed very solemn and even a little disturbed.

"It's not easy for us to say this, Gail." It was Mrs. Omar

31

who spoke now. "But you must bear with us and try to understand that what we're doing is for your own good."

A heavy silence engulfed the room. Then Dr. Omar spoke gently to his daughter, who was looking anxiously at him.

"Gail, dear, your mother and I have made a decision that might seem strange to you, and perhaps will hurt you, but I'm sure only for a little while. When you understand our reasons, I feel sure you will agree that what we're doing is best just now. Our move to New Hampshire and my early retirement has a lot to do with the family. The world is getting more corrupt each day and the cities are becoming more dangerous to live in. The colleges have changed and many new and unpleasant things are taking place there. What we want you to do is to wait—just one year, Gail—before you enroll. Will you give your mother and me one year so we three can enjoy a life of freedom and fun doing things together? After you have gone, it will be too late. So we have withdrawn your name from the freshman class at Skidmore to make room for someone else. If you still want to go the following year, we promise not to object to your decision."

Gail stared at her father in bewilderment, her eyes reflecting shock and dismay.

"You just wouldn't do that to me, would you? Not to go to college with the rest of the kids! I would be a year behind. Is this the reward I get for honor grades, for working so hard to get into the college of my choice? I don't understand what's happening. First you are going to take me away from the home and friends I love and move me to some wilderness and then you deprive me of going to college. Please tell me it isn't so."

"But it is, Gail. It is so. Now, be a good girl and try to

consider it. You'll be more ready for college later. Try to understand that it's your best interest we have at heart."

"My best interest!" Gail jumped up from her chair and faced her father. "I shall never understand that . . . never! And you talk about it as calmly as you would announce that you're not coming home for dinner. I'm not a little girl anymore. How could you even dream that I would understand or that I would agree? Don't you realize that I can think for myself and that *I* have feelings and desires? Just because the world has gone bad for you, you think you can hide me among the mountains. Don't you understand that this is the only world I have to live in? It's the world you have handed down to me, and I like it. I like my world and going to college is part of that world. But what choice do I have? You and Mom have made the decision for me."

Dr. Omar reached out to draw his daughter to him, but she backed away from his touch. He tried to reason with her.

"We knew you would be disappointed at first and that you may hurt for a while, Gail, but we'll make up for it. Just give us a chance. I'll buy you a riding horse, all your own, and we'll have a dog for you to run with. And look at the parties you can have in the winter when your friends come up to ski. They'll think you're the luckiest girl in the world."

"I don't want any parties up there in that old house! And I don't want a horse or a dog! You can't buy me things to replace my not going to college! I can't believe it."

Gail held back the tears that threatened to flow, as she rushed out of the room, grabbing her coat from the hall closet.

"I'm going to Fran's and I will be home at ten," she

announced as she ran out the front door. And before her parents had time to reply, she was halfway down the street in the drizzle and fog.

Gail walked fast. Usually she did not act so impulsively, but this was too much. She just could not stay in that room another moment. To see Fran was the only solution she could think of right now. Perhaps in some way Fran could help. She might ask *her* parents to talk to the Omars. Maybe they could make them understand the injustice of it all. Fran would think of something, for after all, Fran Sawyer was Gail's best friend, and Fran was going to Skidmore, too.

Bravely, Gail put those silly tears in their place; she was simply not going to cry. There must be a way, she kept telling herself over and over again until she stood on the Sawyers' doorstep ringing the bell.

Fran herself opened the door.

"Why Gail!" she exclaimed. "This is mental telepathy. I was just going to call you about Cindy's after-graduation party. You are invited, Gail!"

"Oh, Fran, I don't care about the party. I don't care about anything. My heart is broken into little pieces. You'll never guess what my parents have done to me."

"Come on in the living room," said Fran. "My parents have gone out to dinner tonight, so I'm home alone. We can talk right here."

The girls curled up on the sofa, facing each other, taking advantage of the fact that they had the house to themselves.

Fran brushed the hair from her friend's face.

"You look terrible, Gail!"

"I *feel* terrible, Fran! You couldn't guess what my dear parents have done to me, not in a million years. They have withdrawn my acceptance from Skidmore! Fran, I am not to go to college. I am to stay home and be a good girl and walk dogs and ride horses at a little old country retreat in New Hampshire. They've flipped, but that is the story."

Fran just stared at Gail as if she could not believe the words. Her eyes grew wider and wider.

"But why, Gail? Why? Everyone goes to college! What will happen to you?"

"I don't know, but I am not going to accept it. I am going to do something and I need your help. What would *you* do?"

"I'd run away from home. *My* parents would certainly not whisk me away somewhere, I can tell you that."

"They think they're doing it because they love me."

"That's selfish love, Gail! They just don't want to let you grow up. That's the worst kind. They'll do anything to keep you dependent on them. It's almost like they don't trust you."

"Well, they're not going to succeed. I think I'll run away, Fran, but where will I run to?"

"Maybe you could talk it over with Lynn. She's moving to California, you know, and she's going to college out there. I bet her folks would let you go with them."

"Maybe we should talk it over with her. She always seems to know what to do."

"You poor kid. You really got a dirty deal. I'll do anything I can to help you, Gail. You know that."

"Oh, Fran, if only I knew what to do . . . I do love my parents. Both Mom and Dad are wonderful people, but something weird has happened to Dad. Maybe in time he'll change, but then it will be too late for me to go to Skidmore."

The girls sat silently for a while—two forlorn youngsters delving deep into their own minds to find a solution to Gail's problem. Then Gail looked at her watch.

"It's almost ten o'clock, Fran. I've got to go home."

"Time certainly went fast tonight. I didn't even get a chance to play my new record for you."

"I wasn't in the mood, anyway. See you at school tomorrow."

At 3:00 A.M. Gail was still sitting in a bedroom chair where she had dropped down the moment she had entered her room earlier. She was not conscious of the time. When she came home, she had hurried past the living room where her parents were still sitting.

"How about a cup of hot chocolate, Gail?" her mother had called as she ran up the stairs.

"No, thanks. I don't want anything. I just want to be alone."

That was hours ago. It might have been an eternity. She couldn't make herself go to bed—not while the pain still stabbed her heart. She felt different than she had ever felt before—kind of numb. It had been a strange night. Then, as she sat there hopelessly, she began to think of Grandmother Olsen. Oh, how she wished her grandmother were still alive because *she* would have known just what Gail should do.

Gail had been shocked when her grandmother died last year without warning. Grandmother Olsen had always been such a part of her life, especially after she had moved from Minnesota to live near her only daughter, Barbara, in Lexington. Her grandmother had kept a cute little apartment in a quiet part of town and there she had reigned like a queen. Everything was in perfect order in her few tiny rooms, and there was always the aroma of something very special cooking. Gail could never think of her grandmother as old, because her eyes had always been shining, full of fun and mischief. Her mother had told Gail that she resembled her grandmother both in looks and manner and that had made Gail happy and proud. Often Grandmother Olsen had talked about Norway where she was born and how she had come to America as a young immigrant, finding work in a wealthy household where she had learned to speak English and to do things the American way. Then she had met Peter Olsen, a skilled cabinetmaker, and had fallen completely in love with him. After they were married, they had built a little house on the outskirts of Minneapolis. She had called it Little Scandinavia because there were so many people from her own part of the world living there. Even at the end she had spoken with a slight accent, different from any Gail had ever heard.

After Grandfather had passed away, Mrs. Olsen had moved to Lexington. Her religious faith was firm and true and she knew that she would meet her Peter again in eternity. She often had talked with Gail about that.

"Life here on earth, Gail," she had said when they had walked through the park together one autumn day when the leaves were falling, "is a school, training us for the life to come. That is why the way we live our years on earth is so important. What God has planned for those who believe in Him is so glorious that one could never describe it in mere words. But there is no fear in my heart as I grow older. You see, I am growing nearer and nearer to eternal youth."

Then another time she had said, "Gail, the greatest gift I could ever give to you is the gift of faith—but *I* can't give it. God gives that when you ask to become His child. That's what I want for you more than anything in life. Never forget that if you are lonely, God is your best friend and you can always call upon Him."

Then she had looked out the window as if her eyes were searching the sky.

"God's love is as wide as the ocean, as deep as the sea, and as high as the heavens. And still, my dear, He is as close to you as your own thoughts. It is a mystery that only faith can understand."

Gail could see her grandmother now, in her mind's eye, in these early morning hours when her loneliness was deeper than ever—that dear face, round and rosy-cheeked, almost free of wrinkles, and those clear, bright blue eyes, so filled with love. Oh, how she needed to talk to her grandmother right now.

One summer Dad had rented a lovely cottage on Cape Cod, right on the water, and Grandmother had stayed with them for a whole month. They had spent many an hour walking the beach together, barefooted on the soft sand. Hand in hand they had walked. Gail could not have been more than ten years old then, and Grandmother and her mother and dad had been her whole world. But now Grandmother had left them and Gail had grown up. Her parents were still very dear to her, but little by little, she seemed to grow apart from them. Her friends—Fran, Lynn, and Cindy—seemed to be closer to her now and it was with them that she shared her joys and sorrows. She wondered if that would have happened if Grandmother were still here. When Grandmother died, Gail had lost that beautiful faith they had discussed, and she had grown away from thinking of God as a friend. None of the kids ever mentioned Him.

But tonight Gail tried to pray. She knew she must get some rest. So before she crept into her bed, at 3:30 A.M., she knelt by the chair and for the first time that night she let those blinding tears come. It felt good to let them out. She felt like a little girl again and growing up was an awful task. Life was not beautiful, but full of trouble, disappointment, and, she guessed, danger, like Dad had said. She knelt for a long time without saying a word, just letting the tears flow. Then she spoke in a whisper from a heart that had already found release from its tension.

Dear God, forgive me for forgetting You for such a long time. Now I don't even know if You are real, but You were when Grandmother Olsen was here. Is she with You now? Tell her I want that faith she told me about. I need it because I feel so lonely and lost. Forgive me for thinking badly of Mom and Dad. I know now it is not right. I want to be Your child. Please help me, for I am just a lost teen-ager. Amen.

Then it seemed to Gail that God moved toward her out of the gloom. All was calm within her. She felt washed and cleansed of those disturbing thoughts. There was still so much to be happy about. She would try to understand her parents and try to wait patiently. Soon she would be truly adult and she could choose her own path, and the future might have wonderful things in store for her. Life was full of mysteries. Perhaps she could do something genuinely worthwhile for the world, something that would help other people, especially other teen-agers. Maybe she should be a nurse, helping sick people. Would that please God? Her mind was becoming a little confused—one part of her wanted this, another wanted something else. There was a struggle, she thought, between the real and the unreal. But she could close her eyes and sleep now and see Grandmother Olsen smiling at her. And in the morning she would tell Fran that she had decided to abide by her parents' decision, for she was sure that was what her grandmother would have told her to do.

But in the morning when the alarm rang, Gail's eyes were so heavy she could hardly open them. For a moment she let her thoughts wander back over the previous night's events, but all those lofty thoughts had disappeared. She had been silly and emotional and she was sure that if there were a God, He would never have paid any attention to her prayer. Grandmother Olsen was gone forever and her beautiful philosophy, too. Gail had to live in the present, and that included attending Skidmore. She could not share last night's outburst with Fran, who would just laugh at her. Good old solid Fran! No, she would never tell anyone how childish she had been. This was a new day. Things might not have changed, but no one could take her dearest dreams from her. To be away from home living in a dorm with the other girls, to come and go as she pleased, to be a part of the world no matter how bad it seemed, those were her desires.

She was sullen at breakfast, but her parents did not seem to notice. They discussed the news and their schedules for the day. Never once did they mention the talk they had had with her the night before. Her dad left for the hospital and her mother gathered together the breakfast dishes, humming a gay tune in the kitchen. Somehow that irritated Gail as she collected her books and left for school. She gave her mother a light kiss on the cheek as she passed her.

"Have a happy day, Gail," said Mrs. Omar, smiling.

"You too, Mom."

Gail closed the door behind her and walked down the street. She waved to Fran who was waiting for her on the corner.

4

Barbara Omar was sitting on the edge of the wishing well at Golden Acre. The well was constructed of flat granite, an impressive structure with a round wooden cover tied to one end of a rope, the other end of which was tied to a tree branch. Inside the well, suspended on a crank, was an old wooden bucket.

It was late June and the Omars had been in New Hampshire just one week. Barbara had been drawn to this spot immediately, knowing it would be her favorite. The wishing well had been one of the first things to be restored, and to Barbara, just the sight of it was priceless. She did not really believe in its magic, but the temptation to believe was so strong that she even dropped pennies in it, making wishes, just for fun. She had dropped a coin in the well every day since they had moved in, and even though she laughed at herself for doing it, the mystery and fun always overpowered her logic.

This morning when Barbara had dropped the penny in the well, she had made a special wish for Gail. Barbara's heart was troubled over the change in Gail these last few

months. She had not been the same since the night that
Ernest had told her that they had withdrawn her name
from the freshman class at Skidmore. Oh, she was sweet
and polite, entering obediently into family projects, but
the real Gail—the carefree, happy Gail who had always
been the joy of the family—was gone. Time and time
again Barbara had asked herself if the decision she and
her husband had forced on their daughter had been the
wrong one. The whole question was beginning to wear
on Barbara's nerves, and she knew that she would have to
have a long talk with Ernest. But every time she tried to
bring up the subject, her husband had quieted her fears
and convinced her again that what they had done was
right and that soon Barbara would see the results for
herself.

"Just give her time, Barb," he had said calmly. "Everything is so new to Gail right now. There have been so
many changes. She has to get used to our new way of life.
Young people have a way of adjusting to life whatever
way it turns, and before summer is over, we'll have our
old gal back again."

Barbara hoped so, but on this beautiful morning she
was more unsure than ever. The closeness that had existed between mother and daughter was gone and, of late,
it seemed that Gail actually avoided her company.

But this summer morning was too nice to spend worry-
ing. All of nature seemed to rejoice in its beauty; it was as
if time had stopped. Barbara found it hard to believe that
not so very far away were the cities, hustling and bustling
with activity and people, pushing and rushing to and fro.
Here not a leaf on a tree moved as the sun peeked up from
behind the mountains, throwing its first rays on the dew-
drenched lawn. Barbara's heart warmed to think that this
was their very own plot of land—the soft green grass, the

tall pine and spruce, the green maple. The scent of the pines filled the air—fresh and clean—a balm for one's soul. Then the birds began their twittering, and now and then the chirping melted into a beautiful melody. A rabbit scampered across the lawn, and by the lake two deer came to drink at the shore's edge.

Barbara had awakened at daybreak and followed her urge to go to the wishing well. The world, it seemed to Barbara, was most beautiful in the early morning.

From the house came the aroma of frying bacon. Ernest, too, must have awakened early and not felt like staying in bed. Or could it be Gail? Barbara's heart stood still for a moment. How she hoped it was Gail. She hurried across the lawn to the house.

But it was not Gail. It was Ernest, covered by a king-sized cook's apron, fixing breakfast at the stove.

"Meet your new chef, Mrs. Omar," Ernest laughed as Barbara entered the kitchen. "I woke up early and your side of the bed was empty. Through the window I saw you at the wishing well. Happy morning, hon!"

"Happy morning to you, too! I was almost tempted to wake you and ask you to go with me into the garden, but then I remembered that you still need a lot of rest; so I feasted on the beauty of the morning by myself. This is the most breathtaking morning I can ever remember. Ern, our Golden Acre is a paradise. We have found perfection in life at its fullest."

"And now let's breakfast on the porch facing the lake, if that's all right with you. Just sit down and dream while I finish fixing breakfast."

Barbara sat down on a kitchen chair. It was fun watching Ernest cook. She watched his strong, white hands turning the bacon on the grill—when it struck her. His hands were so beautiful and quick and so skillful in saving human lives. Was it right for them to cease such an awesome task? He was still a man in his prime. Ernest Omar was a handsome man and now with his face relaxed and free from strain, he belied his forty-eight years. Could happiness grow out of selfishness, she wondered. But in a moment Barbara chased these annoying thoughts away. Her husband had spent many years under great tension and the struggle to cope with a changing world had been too much for him. Of course they had a right to take their share of happiness. Those hands had done their duty for mankind.

"I think I hear Gail stirring in her room, Barb," said Ernest. "Let's call her to have breakfast with us."

That morning as the three of them sat around the porch table, the food tasted better than ever. And even Gail seemed to enter into the conversation wholeheartedly. For the first time since they moved to New Hampshire, she seemed more like her old self.

"Did you know that those two black-and-white birds on the lake are loons?" asked Gail. "Mrs. Briggs told me about them. They have lived on that lake for years. She says that loons are almost extinct now. How lucky we are to have two of them."

"We are lucky indeed, Gail," smiled Barbara. "And we also have our wishing well. Have you made a wish yet?"

"No, I don't believe in wishing wells, Mom."

"Oh, it's just for fun, dear. This morning I threw in a penny and made a happy wish for you."

"Thanks, Mom. I need it. You let me know if it comes true."

But later on that morning when Barbara suggested that Gail go with her into town to pick out some furniture for her room, her daughter crept back into a shell.

"I really don't care to go, Mom. You pick out whatever you like."

"But I wanted it to be your choice."

"It doesn't matter, Mom. I just don't care. Whatever you pick out will be fine. You know what goes with the house."

Barbara drove into town alone and chose a colonial bedroom suite with a four-poster canopied bed and a double dresser with a big mirror. She also bought ruffled curtains as white as snow and pink lamps to go with the wallpaper. And when the furniture came, they removed the old pieces and Gail's room looked like a magazine picture. But Gail showed no excitement about it. She just thanked her mother and said it was nice. If Barbara felt let down, she did not let Gail see it. Time after time she reminded herself that her daughter was not herself and that she, her mother, would have to accept that fact until the day she could hear Gail laugh, happy and carefree, the way she used to be.

Often that summer, Barbara let her mind wander back to their last month in Massachusetts and Gail's graduation from high school. The event had been very impressive. Gail had looked so very special in her cap and gown when she received the highest honors in her class. She and Ernest had been so proud to be her parents that night, to see Gail singled out from the other students to give the valedictory speech. But later that night when they had told Gail how happy this had made them, she just gave them a tortured look, a look that had almost broken Barbara's heart.

"What difference does it make now," was all Gail had said and both Barbara and Ernest had gotten her message.

Even that special boyfriend who had escorted Gail to the prom and to Cindy's after-graduation party had not brought happiness to Gail. At times she had looked crushed and resigned when she should have been looking radiant. And behind it all was her disappointment at not going to Skidmore—that wound they had inflicted on her—which now resulted in her apathy about their new home. If only Gail could share her mother's happiness.

Even though Barbara had been very tired from all the packing and from the flurry of parties and dinners given in their honor, she was too happy to let it get her down. She was particularly glad she had given a luncheon for Gail's closest friends the week before they moved. Barbara had given its preparation all her artistic skill, and even if Gail did not say anything about it, in her heart she must have realized how much her mother wanted her to be happy. But the summer was passing, and she did not seem to be any more content.

Then one day Barbara was much encouraged when Gail suddenly announced that she would climb the hill to the Briggs's house to get a little better acquainted with their neighbors.

"They will love having you come, Gail," Barbara beamed. "Why don't you invite them here for dinner tomorrow night? I'd like to know them better, too. They are so dear and so alone."

"Oh, let's wait a while before we ask them down, Mom. We don't want to force ourselves on them too soon."

"Perhaps you're right, dear. Well, we can wait a couple of weeks. We have the whole summer ahead of us."

The first Sunday the Omars had attended the Community Church, a few miles down the road, they found to their surprise that every seat was filled. But at the door, the beaming middle-aged preacher told them, as they shook his hand, that it was only in the summer that he had the joy of preaching to a full house.

"It's the vacationers," he said. "In the wintertime I have only a handful of faithful members who come to worship."

The church building was of modest size with old-fashioned pews. The small choir consisted of untrained but enthusiastic voices and the organist beat the time with her head while she played.

The Omars discussed the church on their way home.

"It is a dear church," said Barbara, "and so near to our Golden Acre. We should be a part of it and perhaps we can be of some help. I would love to sing in the choir. How about adding our voices to the rest?"

"Not me!" protested Gail. "If you join, count me out. Why, there's no one there under forty."

"Well, we'll just think about it," said Barbara. "I think it would be good to be a part of the little church since our roots are going to be planted here among these people."

Later that Sunday they packed a picnic lunch and drove their station wagon up a narrow dirt road. Up and up it went until they found themselves on a plateau on the mountaintop. For a moment they stood breathlessly looking down over the valley below. The view was a joy to behold, and the gurgling of a small waterfall running down the mountainside was music to their ears. In this pure air they set up their portable picnic table and unpacked the basket.

"Food certainly tastes better eaten in surroundings like these," Doctor Omar proclaimed. "I have never dined at a more beautiful eating place."

Barbara and Gail agreed. And, Barbara thought, to start

a new life, they could not have found a more beautiful setting in God's wonderful world.

It was growing dark when they returned home and it was then that Gail brought up the subject of the curse.

"You never told me about it," she said, "and the Briggses thought I knew. They are really worried about us."

Ernest Omar laughed heartily. "Oh, Gail, there was really nothing to tell. The curse is a silly way of explaining accidents that have happened to people. I never thought of telling you about it."

"But to the Briggses it is very real," insisted Gail. "If you believe in wishing wells, how can you ignore curses?"

"I never believed in wishing wells," said Dr. Omar. "That is Mom's fancy. But you just wait and see, Gail. When nothing bad comes our way, everyone will know there is no curse."

"*Amen* to that!" agreed Barbara.

After Gail had gone into the house, Ernest and Barbara sat on the broad front steps, still talking about the curse.

"What if this place really is cursed?" asked Barbara.

Darkness moved over the land and Barbara moved closer to her husband.

"Barb," he said gently, "don't tell me that you are beginning to believe that silly curse, too."

"I don't really, but when darkness falls over the mountain, it gives me an eerie feeling, and tonight I feel a strange fear creeping up on me. Everything is almost too perfect and I want so much for it all to stay beautiful."

"It will, darling."

Ernest placed his arm around his wife's shoulders.

"You see, only our own minds can change beauty and peace into ugliness and fear," he said. "So please, dear, don't brood about it."

But the silence that had been so soothing in the sunshine suddenly made her uneasy. Heavy shadows hung over Golden Acre and the trees and bushes took on weird, ugly shapes and the call of the loons on the lake seemed a bad omen. The whole scene was like a warning, a prophecy that perfect happiness could not survive in today's world. Hand in hand, they walked into their lovely home, and Barbara, for the first time, felt a twinge of homesickness for the old house in Lexington. She missed the noise of the city streets, the lights and neon signs, and the friends and activities which had filled her days in Boston.

Most of all, she missed the old Gail. It *was* fun for them all, back in Lexington. Although she and Ernest used to marvel at the never-ending procession of their daughter's friends, and how they could sit for hours giggling over Cokes and pretzels about youthful confidences and plans for school clubs, rallies, and other projects, they had been proud that Gail was a doer. It was refreshing and gratifying to them as parents that she was such a vibrantly alive member of her generation, and that she had always shared her enthusiasm for life with them. It was a special pleasure to see her joy about college, and how it was going to help her carve her niche in a sometimes disturbing, but, to Gail, vitally alive society.

Here at Golden Acre, Gail was subdued, aloof, and even secretive. She took long walks, and often could be found dreamily gazing into the distant hills from her favorite retreat down where the brook whispered over the rocks. Gail seldom mentioned her friends, although Barbara knew that many letters were exchanged. There were young people in town and youth activities at the church, but any efforts to get her interested in them met with a quiet, though polite, rejection. Wasn't it really unnatural for Gail to be so placid and accepting about the change in her college plans? It actually would have been less disturbing if she had continued to openly express her disappointment, than take the passive attitude she did now. Strange that she never brought up the subject since that spring evening when she was so upset about their decision for her future.

But summer moved on, and many guests dropped in to see their paradise and to spend a few days taking trips up into the mountains. Barbara's fears on that strange night of foreboding were completely forgotten. All was calm now and evenings were beginning to cool. Soon they would need extra blankets on their beds at night. August had come and the days were still warm and sunny. The house repairs were almost completed and earlier that month they had freshened the outside paint. Now the soft golden yellow of the house truly matched its name. It was really becoming, like a bright spot of sunlight in all the greenery. They picked wild blueberries in the woods and Barbara froze as many as she could get into the new freezer—to be enjoyed in the cold winter months. Never had a summer passed more quickly, and never had a few months been more filled with peace, love, security, and simple joys.

Still . . . late in August Barbara began to notice a certain wistfulness and restlessness in Gail. She knew so well why—this was the time Gail should have been getting ready for college and although Gail never mentioned it, her mother guessed that Gail's heart was aching and Barbara's, too, was filled with pain and regret.

Barbara was now convinced that withdrawing Gail's name had been a grave mistake. Gail would never be happy if she could not follow her own heart's desire. Perhaps, Barbara thought, after this summer of rest, Ernest would see it that way. If not, she must convince him, and soon!

One day Barbara placed a phone call to the college admissions office and to her great relief, there were two vacancies due to recent cancellations. Barbara had a week to give them a final answer and although her mind was already made up, she would have at least that much time to convince Ernest that they had acted too hastily. Now they could make it up!

This afternoon Ernest was fishing on the lake. She could see the small boat gliding along on the water. He had been fishing for hours, so evidently the fish were not biting. This would not be the time to approach him. Barbara walked to the edge of the water.

"How's the fishing going, dear?" she called out.

"Not very well today, Barb. I haven't had even a bite for the last hour. I'm coming in if you'll wait there—I've had enough for today."

Barbara waited, but decided not to discuss Gail's college. When Ernest did not catch any fish, he was never in a good mood; but tomorrow she would bring it up. She was sure she could persuade him to her way of thinking. After all, he loved Gail as much as she did. She imagined the happiness returning to Gail's face when they told her the good news. Then she and Gail would go shopping and plan and pack and all would be well once more for all of them. This was the greatest gift they could give their daughter.

Barbara was gay as she and Ernest crossed the lawn to the house.

"My, you are happy this afternoon, Barb," he remarked. "You look like you just inherited a million dollars."

"I did," laughed Barbara. "Not in money, but in peace of mind."

If Ernest had asked her to share her happiness at that time, life might have taken a different course, but Dr. Omar just smiled at his pretty wife and went to put away his fishing gear. Surely she could wait until the morrow to say what she had to say, Barbara decided.

That night when Gail was ready for bed and came to say good-night to her mother, it seemed to Barbara that she looked at her strangely, as if there were something she wanted to tell her mother. For a moment Barbara almost revealed her own secret plans, but loyalty to her husband forbade it. First she must discuss it with him, and then she could tell Gail. So instead she just hugged her very tightly.

"You are very dear to me, Gail," she said. "Always remember that."

"You are dear to me, too, Mom." Gail's eyes shimmered as though they were filling with tears. "Always remember that, too," she whispered. "Always, Mom—no matter what happens, remember I love you."

Why, it was like old times, thought Barbara. These were just like the little endearments they used to exchange.

It had thrilled Barbara's mother-heart, for it had been such a long time since that close feeling existed between them. And soon Ernest would be included in the closeness, and nothing would make him happier than to have his girl back again.

That night, after they all had retired, Barbara felt that a heavenly benediction rested over their Golden Acre. All was well and no curse could ever touch them now.

5

Gail Omar was scared! She was not, by nature, bold, and just now she felt very young and unsure of herself. But she had great determination and an unwielding loyalty toward her friends. What Gail was about to do now had been decided months ago, even before she left Lexington, by Fran and Lynn and herself in the recreation room of Lynn's basement. Fran had called it a conference. A major decision had to be made, finding a solution to Gail's disastrous dilemma. This discussion took place only a few days after Gail had come to Fran's house in tears, sharing with her best friend her parents' decision not to let her enter Skidmore in the fall.

The basement room had been a perfect setting for their confidential talk. The girls were assured that they would not be disturbed and had talked to their hearts' content.

"As I said before, Gail," Fran had said, "you have to run away from home. It's best to be as dramatic as you can."

"But I'm chicken," sighed Gail. "I wouldn't know how to go about it. It scares me to death just thinking about it."

"When the time comes, you can do it," Lynn had said,

giving Gail a pat on the arm. "Come to California. I'll be there by then, and I'll see that you have a place to stay. My parents are great. We could tell them, and then you might be able to stay with us. But I'll have to sound them out first, before I can promise. They might feel obligated to tell your parents."

"But I'll have to work before I can go to college. I might even have to go to school at night. What work can I do? I'm not trained for anything and I've never worked before."

"You can always do something like baby-sitting or working in a store. You don't need training for that. But you'll have to get a Social Security card and that might take a little time."

"By the way," asked Fran, "do you have any money of your own? You can't run away without money."

"Yes, I have my own bank account and I have almost one thousand dollars in it. It was put in my name this year so I could draw from it when I was away at college. I can take some money out of that."

"You should have six or seven hundred dollars," said Lynn. "Better put it in traveler's checks. Then you'll have nothing to worry about until you start earning some yourself."

"I'll do that before we move," said Gail. "I can always tell the bank it's for college. I'm game for anything as long as I can get away from home."

"You mustn't hitchhike though," Lynn had said, "unless it's to get to a train or airport or bus. And don't go anywhere near Boston. That's the first place your folks would try to find you."

There had been much to talk about that night, but when the girls had parted, they had everything settled. Gail knew that in mid-August, on a certain day or night, she would leave her new home for an unknown world. But her final destination would be Los Angeles where she would meet with Lynn and make further plans. That evening had been an exciting one and when the girls left they had sworn each other to secrecy.

But now the time had come. Half the month of August was past and many letters had been exchanged, and Lynn was now in California eagerly awaiting her friend's arrival. Lynn had decided it would be best to leave her parents out of it, until Gail's arrival on the coast. Gail had destroyed all their correspondence so that no clues were left behind. Gail's traveler's checks had long been hidden in the lining of her trench coat and all was ready. Now, on the next day, the fifteenth of August, she would leave. Even the weather report was favorable. If it had been for rain, she would have delayed just one more day. She was taking only a minimum of necessary clothing in a rather large tote bag, and for some inexplicable reason, when she checked it for the last time, she had tucked in a small white Bible, her last gift from Grandmother Olsen. At daybreak she would set off, leaving a note on her pillow saying that she had climbed the hills.

"If I am late getting home, drive up to the Briggses," she had written, hating the implied lie.

There would be hills to climb as she hiked along, and it was important for her parents to contact Mrs. Briggs, for that was where she had left her real message, although Mrs. Briggs had no idea that she had it.

Gail had become quite friendly with Mr. and Mrs. Briggs, and she knew that they enjoyed her visits. Perhaps, in some small way, her visits made up for the loss of the grandchildren they might have had by now if their own daughter had lived. The last visit with Mrs. Briggs had been fun, and they had sat on the wide porch talking when Gail had handed her a gaily wrapped package, tied with a bright ribbon.

"This is for Mom, Mrs. Briggs," Gail had said. "I have a very special reason for wanting you to give it to her instead of me doing it."

"Am I keeping it for a reason?" Mrs. Briggs had asked.

"I don't want Mom to find it before that important day, and you know about mothers. They do snoop around."

"I'll be glad to help you out, Gail. Is it her birthday?"

"No, but we celebrate all sorts of silly occasions in our family. We don't have to have a birthday to receive a special gift—and this has to be given on a particular day."

"You don't have to explain, my dear. Your package will be safe with me until you tell me to give it to your mom."

"It won't be long. Some afternoon Mom and Dad will come driving up the hill and stop to ask if I am here. That's the day you will give her the package and tell her it's from me."

"You don't have to worry, Gail. I'll do exactly as you wish. The surprise is quite safe with me."

Gail had agonized over her decision that day as she walked down the hill toward home. The little white box, so brightly wrapped, contained a sad present, a gift that would break her mother's heart, and her father's, too. Inside there was a letter written and rewritten many times before Gail was satisfied. A teardrop had fallen, leaving a small stain on her signature. When Gail went to bed that night, she envisioned the letter—every word imprinted on her brain.

Dear Mom,

As I climbed the hill today to leave this letter with Mrs. Briggs, my heart was heavy. Mrs. Briggs thinks

it is a gift for you. Please understand that it pains me
to hurt you, but I feel I must step out into the world to
do my own thing.

My world is not the one you are hiding from, and I
want to face it and learn to live in it unafraid. I can't
bear the thought of spending a winter here in the
wilderness. I need my friends, and I miss them so
much and I miss the life I used to lead. So, I am
leaving to start out to seek my own way. I promise
that if I feel I am wrong, I'll be back before you know
it, and I know you will forgive me for trying.

Please don't worry about me. I have drawn some
money from my bank account, and I will travel until I
find some work to finance me in college somewhere.
Don't try to find me. Let me do this *my way*, please. I
am not a little girl anymore, and I hope you know I
am levelheaded and will not do anything foolish.
When I have found my way, I will get in touch.

I love you very much. Have fun on your Golden
Acre; I can't feel that it's mine. Even if this might
seem to you like the beginning of that curse, as you
yourself said, it is only our own thoughts that can
make it so.

Lovingly,

GAIL

Gail's alarm rang at 4:00 A.M. She rubbed her sleepy
eyes and jumped out of bed. The house was very still.
Quickly she dressed and made her bed, placing the note
on her pillow. She picked up her room so it was orderly.
Alongside her tote bag was the lunch which she had made
the night before. It contained a few sandwiches and a big
red apple. Gail tied a scarf around her blond hair and
slipped on her trench coat. The morning would be chilly

in spite of the fact that it was still summer by the calendar. Noiselessly she made her way down the stairs and out the back door and began her trek to the highway. She took one long last look at the house and threw a kiss toward her parents' room.

Gail did not feel very brave this morning. The tears were there just behind her eyelids, but she held them back. This was not the time for crying. She walked along quickly. The morning air felt good and the dew-drenched grass glistened as the sun came out bright and clear from behind the mountains. Her heart was filled with strange emotions as she tried to put thoughts of home and parents behind her. But no matter how hard she tried, the thoughts stormed her mind. She wondered if on this very morning Mom had arisen early and sat by the wishing well, dropping in a penny and wishing for her daughter's happiness. She wondered if her dad was cooking breakfast. If so, then soon he would go to her room and find the note. He would be glad thinking she had found pleasure in climbing the hills, believing that she had begun to really enjoy the mountains at last. Mom and Dad would laugh about it while they ate their breakfast in peace, having no idea what that day would bring. It would be afternoon before they drove up the hill to the Briggses and by then she would be far, far away, she hoped.

In her imagination, Gail could see Mrs. Briggs handing Mom the package, while smiling from ear to ear. Her parents would probably not open it until they returned home . . . and then they would find the letter . . . and Mom would cry and Dad would pace the floor back and forth. For a brief moment Gail felt that she could not bear the thought of hurting them, that she had better turn back and return home. But no, she could not stop now! Again she fought back the tears and hurried on along the lonely highway.

A truck came driving up the hill; the truck driver slowed down and leaned out the window.

"Want a lift?" he called.

Gail shook her head. She would not accept a ride from just anyone. She must be sure of the kind of person she traveled with, if she did decide to accept a ride. Her feet were beginning to get tired now, and she slowed her pace and nibbled on one of her sandwiches. There was a small pool by the road; a cup hung on a branch nearby. Gail rinsed out the cup and drank some water. The spring water was cool and pure. Gail began to feel better and some of her apprehension left her. The world was a beautiful place and the birds seemed to be singing just for her. An inner strength lifted her spirits, and for the first time in some months she was herself. She was really doing the very thing that had scared her so, and she found that she had both guts and determination.

Gail wondered if Grandmother Olsen would have approved of what she was doing. In her heart, Gail thought she would have. She could almost see her grandmother's blue eyes twinkling. Yes, Grandmother would have understood why she was doing this, and one day her parents, too, would know she was right.

The sun was high now, but there was still very little traffic. Mainly trucks passed, but no one else asked if she wanted a ride. She wondered how far it was to the nearest city or town where she could get transportation. Walking did not get you there very fast. Gail laughed aloud. She was free now and on an adventure to a place called *Nowhere*. New Hampshire was beautiful this morning, with its towering mountains and clear blue sky, and she felt she was part of it all. She had no time limit and no ties, just sun and fresh air and the sky. Her feet were walking on and on without really knowing where they were going. Gail was free at last to do whatever she liked with her life. This was the first morning of a new beginning. Gail lifted her face to the sun and slipped off her trench coat and carried it on her arm. Already it was getting warm and it was only 8:00 in the morning.

There was a picnic grove beside the road, and Gail sat down at a table. She would eat the rest of her sandwiches here. She was really hungry. There was only one small sports car parked in the area and a young man sat eating at another table. Gail glanced over at him. He was quite handsome, in his late twenties, with wavy dark hair. As he looked over at Gail, she saw a sparkle in his brown eyes. He wore a light green sweater over a sports shirt. Even as he relaxed on the bench she could sense a quality of energy and vigor. Then he spoke.

"Hey, what did you do with your car? I was sitting here alone meditating on the beauty of the morning when I looked around and there you were sitting at the next table. Did you drop out of the sky?"

Gail laughed. "I have no car. I'm walking. You see, I come from *No Place* and *Nowhere*'s my destination."

"That sounds interesting! Do you mind if I move over so we can have breakfast together?"

"Not if you share a couple of sips of coffee with me."

"You can have a whole cupful. I have more in the car."

In a moment he was sitting beside her.

"Where are you really heading?" he asked, as he poured some coffee for her.

"I told you. I'm going nowhere. I'm off on an adventure. I couldn't go to college this fall, so I'm looking for a job. When I get enough money, I'll find a college. Does that make any sense?"

"Not much, but it might answer my next question. Could I give you a ride part of the way, wherever it is?"

"Yes, I accept. My feet are tired. It's kind of you. Thanks."

"Let me introduce myself. I'm Douglas Rhodes from Vermont, just across the New Hampshire line, and I'm headed for Pennsylvania to a little town called Earthend. It's no more than a pinprick on the map, but there the people will call me Pastor Rhodes. I've just been ordained and I'm going to my first pastorate."

Gail's eyes opened wide.

"Now I really feel safe riding with you."

Gail laughed, then it dawned on her that she, too, had to give a name, though not her own. But she hesitated only a moment.

"I'm Gail Olsen from New Hampshire."

"Swedish?"

"No, Norwegian."

"I guess I can't hold that against you, but I have many Swedish friends and I'm very fond of them."

"Norwegians have it all over the Swedes."

Douglas Rhodes laughed heartily.

"That's not the way I've heard it. I guess they both claim they are the best."

"I really am not an expert on the subject. I'm only third generation."

"Well, I guess we won't have any trouble since I'm just an ordinary Vermonter."

In a few minutes they were driving away in Douglas's small sports car. It was a treat to Gail to rest her feet. Douglas was a handsome young preacher and very pleasant. What good luck she had had, and now she didn't have to worry about the possibility of her parents catching up with her.

For a while they talked casually about the weather and the beauty of the countryside and the mountains, and then there was silence, not an awkward silence, but a peaceful one, with just the hum of the tires as they put mile after mile behind them. Gail felt her eyes close. She had been up so early, and all that walking had really made her tired. She leaned her head back and before she knew it, she had drifted off to sleep.

6

Gail Omar kept her eyes closed. She was captivated by a strange new feeling and for a moment she cared about neither time nor distance. She had no idea how long she had been riding with Douglas Rhodes in his car. It might have been hours, days, or weeks. She just felt a secure sense of well-being; all was well with her and the world. The struggle within her had subsided; Gail felt at peace. If this was a spell she was under, she did not want to break it, and she was sure that would happen if she opened her eyes. So she willed herself to dream that this journey with her new companion would never end, and that when they reached Earthend, Pennsylvania, Doug would ask her to stay on. Was she in love? Could she have fallen in love in such a short time with someone she knew nothing about? Whatever it was, it was like a tremendous force holding her pleasantly captive.

Through half-closed eyes, Gail watched Doug Rhodes sitting at the wheel, his eyes trained on the road with the air of a careful driver. His dark hair curled at the lobe of his ear. His eyelashes were long and thick, his chin firm and determined—certainly a strong chin, Gail decided. She knew that he was tall and slim and that his eyes were a soft brown that sometimes twinkled when he spoke. His voice was deep, with a catch in it that made her heart beat a little faster. Yes, Douglas Rhodes was a handsome young man. But why had he chosen to become a preacher, Gail wondered. He certainly didn't look like the few she had met.

Just then the young man turned to her and smiled.

"How long are you going to play possum with me?" he asked, teasingly. "I know you're awake, but for some reason you're keeping your eyes closed. You haven't been asleep for some time."

Gail laughed out loud.

"So, I've been discovered! I was playing a game. Do you want to know what it was? I was playing that I belonged in this car and that I was accompanying you to Earthend. But don't pay any attention to me; I'm great at playing games."

Now it was Doug's turn to laugh.

"You're a strange little girl, but you are honest and I like that. If you want to ride all the way, it's okay with me. I just don't know what you will do when you get to Earthend. It's the most Godforsaken place you've ever seen. I don't even know if there's a bus that leaves there or if they have a hotel. But I'm sure you can get a room with one of my parishioners for the night. They are wonderful, kind, solid citizens. I know you'll like them."

"Well, if it's all right with you, I will tag along. As I told you before, I don't know just where I'm headed for yet."

"Well, now that's settled, let's consider another matter. I'm hungry! How about you? Would you like to stop at the next place for lunch?"

"Sure! I'm hungry as a bear myself. But there is one thing . . . I want to pay for my own food."

"That's fine with me if that's the way you feel, but believe me, even if I am a poor preacher, I do have the money to pay for both of us."

"Thank you, but I'll feel better if I take care of my own food. It's enough that I'm riding along on your gasoline."

Hamburgers and Coke had never tasted better to Gail than in that roadside restaurant. She and Doug laughed and talked as they ate and outside the sun was shining on the loveliest August day that Gail could ever remember.

Soon they were back in the car, each with a double-dip ice cream cone to eat on the way. It all seemed like such fun. For just a few moments there was a pleasant silence with only the tires making sound on the pavement.

It was Doug who broke the silence.

"I've been thinking about the hours we still have to travel. Earthend is way up in the mountains so we have a lot of steep climbing to do before we reach our destination. If you want to go to sleep again, it's okay with me."

"No, I'm not a bit sleepy," said Gail. "I would so much rather talk."

"Fine. Talking makes the driving more pleasant. What shall we talk about since we can't talk about you?"

"We can talk about you! I've been wondering why of all professions you chose to be a minister."

"It's a long, long story, and you might be bored."

"No, I really am interested. Would it really take all the time to Earthend to tell it?"

"That depends on whether or not I get in a preaching mood. But I will tell you the story anyway. It's good for me to think back."

"I'll get real comfortable," said Gail and she stretched

back against the seat. "Now I'll get a sample of what kind of a preacher you'll make."

Douglas Rhodes was quiet for a moment, collecting his thoughts. Then he began speaking in a pleasant deep voice.

"You see, Gail, as a boy, I had never even considered the ministry. For as long as I can remember, I wanted to be a doctor—a surgeon, in fact. I wanted to be an outstanding surgeon, one who could remove the sickness from people and make them well. My grandfather was a country doctor, one of the old school who never considered himself when it came to helping those who were suffering. When I say he was a doctor, I mean he was the real thing. His name was never in print for his unselfish work or for the miracles he performed, but I can tell you that he gave his life to help humanity. To him, medicine was not a profession, but a calling."

"He must have been a wonderful doctor," said Gail softly, wishing within herself that she could tell Doug that her own father was also a doctor. Somehow she felt it wiser not to tell even that much about herself.

"To me, when I was a little boy, he came next in line to God. We were real buddies. He let me ride alongside of him in his shiny black Ford and I felt sort of special accompanying him on his sick calls. Of course, I never went in the houses with him. I just sat there in the car, waiting and knowing that someday I would be able to do a job like his, that one day, so far away then, I would be a doctor like he was.

"We talked a lot on our rides, and I told him over and over again that one day I would fill his place. He always gave me a big grin when I talked like that and ruffled my hair and said he was sure he would be very proud of me

when I became a man. And if I became a doctor, I would
surely be a good one, he predicted.

"I shall never forget one noon when we had traveled
about thirty miles to see a very sick old man. We had
stopped on the mountainside to eat our lunch. Grandma
was great at putting up lunches for her two menfolks.
Vermont was at its best that spring day with budding
leaves bursting and a noisy brook spilling down the
mountainside. Gramp handed me a sandwich and poured
me a glass of milk from the thermos. His otherwise jolly
face had a thoughtful look.

" 'Douglas,' he had said, 'there are many things that
you should know about being a doctor that you won't
learn in medical school. The world is full of sick people
looking for help, but sometimes the sickness is not of the
body, but of the soul. Sometimes to hold a hand and place
a cool hand on a forehead gives more relief than a pill.
Sometimes you need just smile and tell them they are
doing fine. You see, there is so much heartache and loneliness in the world. People of all ages are starving for love
and must be given hope for the future and courage to live
through even the dark days. That is why I always carry the
Book with me,' and Gramp held up an old worn Bible. 'In
here,' he continued, 'is all the wisdom you need. This is
God's Word to mankind. I always find the answer here. As
a doctor, I am a mender of bodies, but God is the One who
has charge of the real healing, the giving or taking of life.
Don't ever forget that!' "

Doug turned to Gail. "I still have Gramp's old Bible.
It's mine now," he said simply.

"I have a Bible, too," said Gail. "It belonged to my
grandmother and I have it with me in my tote bag."

The moment Gail had uttered the words she had regretted them. She had been so engrossed in Doug's story that she had forgotten to be on guard about her own past.

But Doug reached out and took her hand, for just a moment. He held it in a firm grip and then, just as quickly, released it.

"Then we have something in common," he said. "Two treasures handed down to us from the older generation."

"Yes," smiled Gail, "and now you know something about me. But keep on with your story."

"Gramp was right. The world is full of sickness and people are lost in their own confusion. Perhaps it was those thoughts that made me begin to think of the ministry. I think that doctors today are too busy to live by Gramp's philosophy. The old country doctors are dying out and I knew I couldn't be like him in this new world . . . but, wait a minute; I forgot to tell you that my grandparents brought me up. I lived with them from the time I was three years old. Both my parents had died and I was an only child. Gramp was Dad's father, so my name was the same as theirs. I always felt I was their son. Anyway, I grew up and went to college, but I never did enter medical school. You see, one weekend when I was home in Vermont, Gramp left early on an urgent sick call. He had a long list of calls that day. I didn't travel with him anymore. I stayed home and did some odd jobs for Grandma.

"He was late coming home, but Grandma kept his dinner hot and we waited until we heard the Ford chugging up the hill. But he never got out of the car. When I went out to see what had happened, I found him slumped over the wheel. His great big wonderful heart had stopped beating. Gramp had left this world like an old sailor, sailing his ship into port for the last time. The world had lost a great man, and I had lost my best friend. No one had ever been closer to me than Gramp.

"Those were sad days as we put him to rest. People came from miles around to bid him farewell. They brought flowers for his grave, but there were few tears. Vermonters don't give themselves over much to visible emotion, yet I knew how their hearts grieved for him. Never would they find another doctor-friend like Dr. Rhodes.

"I knew the world was filled with sick people who needed help, and Gramp had handed me the challenge. But medicine had no allure for me anymore. Instead I was thinking more and more of the ministry, where I could continue Gramp's work of helping the lost and sick and lonely. So I entered theological school—but I didn't find what I was looking for there, either. Perhaps I have a bit of the problem of our generation—I am always looking for something that isn't there. Either it never was or it has been lost in the yesterdays. I found that even many students of theology were not interested primarily in learning to help mankind. They were more interested in big churches and the many benefits of a rosy, secure future. I felt that Gramp would have been proud of me when I finally made my decision. There was nothing to stop me from helping mankind, so I chose to serve a small church in a place where people needed me and where I could give of myself as Gramp had.

"Perhaps that seems self-righteous and noble to you now, but you haven't seen the total picture yet. There's no way to explain it properly; it has to be experienced."

"Is that the end of the story?" asked Gail softly.

"Yes, that's all I have to tell. I wish you would share your own story with me now. I'm sure you have one, too."

Ignoring his silent question, Gail asked one of her own, "You didn't tell me how your grandmother felt about your giving up medicine."

"Well, Grandma somehow understood what I was doing—she knew I had to find my own place. She was very sweet about it when I told her I was taking this little church. She gave me her blessing. She told me to go and preach the Word of God, starting with the Sermon on the Mount, because that contained the key to happiness. And she told me that she knew that Gramp, somewhere in eternity, was proud of me."

"And you really are doing what you wanted, Doug. You are giving yourself to the world. I am sitting here in awe of you! You have some fine ideals and here I am just about to throw away my life. I think you have found your first convert. It's a strange feeling, but I think I'd like to help you with your work up there in the mountains—if you can use me. I have enough money for a time. Do you think I could be of some use in your church?"

"I don't know, Gail. But thank you for your offer. Perhaps we could ask the church elders if I could use a secretary, but you will have to tell me something about yourself before I could consult them. You do understand that, don't you?"

"You know my name and that I want to find a job, that I have a Bible and come from New Hampshire and that I don't want to talk about myself and would like to do something for the world. That's really quite a bit to know about someone."

"Okay, we'll leave it that way for now, and if I can, I'll help you find something worthwhile to do."

"Perhaps I'm sick in my soul, Doug. Maybe I need to have someone hold my hand and assure me that everything is all right. It might help if I tried to be useful."

"I can't promise anything, Gail, but we'll wait and see. I'm glad you have plenty of time."

The silence was heavy now. Doug's last words seemed to be tinged with sarcasm, or perhaps it was just Gail's guilty imagination. Restless thoughts disquieted Gail. She wished now that she had given Doug her right name at the start. Oh, why hadn't she told him about her parents, that she was the daughter of a fine doctor who had worked hard to help mankind? She should have defended the doctors of today. Now her mind was confused. Perhaps if she told him now, it would make matters worse. He might say he could not trust her working in his church. That would break her heart, especially now when she wanted to please him so very much. She had never before met a person as fine and wonderful as Douglas Rhodes. Better to leave things as they were. Perhaps it was destiny that had brought them together on this journey.

It was late afternoon now, and it seemed an eternity since that morning, when she had left Golden Acre. Everything there seemed so far removed. By this time her parents knew that she had gone away. They were probably heartbroken, and perhaps they had set out to try to find her. She was sorry she had caused them sorrow and pain, but she would not have missed meeting this young preacher for anything. Strange that this very morning she had not even known he existed, and he now seemed so important to her.

Gail thought about her Grandmother Olsen. Someday she would tell Doug about her. Her grandmother would have liked Doug. Gail was glad she had brought the little Bible along; it seemed to draw her closer to her grandmother. Then she wondered about Lynn. Would Lynn worry when she did not hear from Gail? It was necessary that she not let anyone know where she was for a while. She'd have to work things out for herself. Neither Fran nor Lynn would understand about Doug or her sudden desire to volunteer her work to help him. Even college didn't seem very important just now.

There were many roads one might take in life. Just finding the right one was very important, and Gail had a feeling that the one she was taking at that moment was *the one* for her. Whatever came of it in the future did not matter, for just now what was important was the warm, secure feeling she felt just sitting in the same car with this young preacher. She thought she would like to stay with him forever.

"Gail Olsen," said Doug suddenly, "I was just thinking. I will have to have some explanation for my church members in Earthend for traveling there with a pretty girl. If I said I had picked her up along the roadside, they might not like it so well, and it would be awkward for all of us. As a preacher, I have to think of my reputation."

"And now I bet you feel that you have to dump me somewhere," sighed Gail.

"No, not at all! I'd like to have you along, but there has to be an explanation. Somehow I feel there is a reason for our meeting."

"I feel that way, too," confessed Gail, "but then what shall we do?"

"You seem like such an honest girl, Gail. I don't know why you are hiding your past so closely, but I am trying to trust you and know that you have a good reason."

Gail squeezed Doug's arm.

"Thanks a million! I promise I'll not let you down."

Just before dark they climbed the last hill to the town of Earthend, Pennsylvania. The view from the mountains was breathtakingly beautiful. Gail thought of the towering peaks she had left in New Hampshire, and their cool beauty, now so far away. One day's journey from mountains to mountains, she was thinking. These mountains did not feel at all ominous, but warm and protective—she would love them.

"I am supposed to drive right to the church," said Doug, "and we will soon be there. The people have prepared a dinner for me somewhere, and I hope to take you along. But I'll have to make up some kind of story. You will have to be my secretary whom I brought along because you wanted to donate your time. I'm sure they will not object. We can be old friends, as far as they know, and I hope the Lord will not charge me with a lie. We do have to arrive in a respectable manner."

"I hope they will like me," said Gail in an anxious voice.

"They can't help but like you," smiled Doug. "Don't be scared. Everything will fall into place."

They had begun to enter the small village. Low houses, some of them a bit dilapidated, but with well-tended gardens, were a delight to Gail's eyes. Every house was seemingly surrounded by flowers in every variety and color. The air was fresh and pure and the sun, sinking in the west, shaded the countryside in gold and purple. Birds twittered merrily in the trees. Here and there she saw people outside their homes, mowing their lawns or weeding their gardens or chatting with neighbors over white fences. Most of them looked elderly. She wondered if there were any young people in town, or whether they had all left for the excitement of the cities. Earthend —how fitting was the name—with its boundary wall of mountains looming over the end of town.

And then she saw the church—a small white building with a spire pointing proudly skyward, its cross in silhouette upon the cloudless blue. It was very tiny. Why it couldn't house even a hundred people, she thought.

"This is my church, Gail," said Doug. "What do you think of it? It has just been painted, I see. The people have really been sprucing it up for me. My church—my very first church. I must stop the car and take a good look at it before we go inside."

For a moment Doug gazed wordlessly at the church. It was as if his eyes measured it carefully from side to side and top to bottom. Then he bowed his head in silent prayer.

What a man, thought Gail, and tears sprang to her eyes. She wondered if the people in this little town knew what a great gift they were receiving from God—the Reverend Douglas Rhodes—grandson of the selfless Dr. Rhodes. Suddenly she found her own heart praying.

Dear God, give him success here. Bless this wonderful man, Thy servant, and crown him with glory as he leads these people in Thy will. Amen.

Doug stepped from the car and opened her door. The church door opened just at that moment, and a plump, matronly woman came down the steps. There was a broad smile on her face as she hurried over and reached out her hand in welcome.

7

The same morning that Gail had left Golden Acre, Barbara Omar had awakened early. She had spent a restless night. What had troubled her mind was how to convince her husband that they had been wrong about Gail's education, that they had broken her heart by denying her the right to enter Skidmore. Then she would have to tell him that she had called the college and been told that there was still an opening for Gail if they acted quickly. Over and over again, Barbara had rehearsed her words—what to say—how to say it. But every time she planned to say something, she changed her mind, thinking that this was not the right moment to approach Ernest. Well, her procrastination had to stop. She would tell him today—this very morning, even before they were out of bed. And after all, perhaps morning would be the best time to speak of a new beginning for their daughter.

Just now it was still very dark, although dawn was about to break in the eastern sky. As she lay there thinking, Barbara thought she heard something moving about in the house. The sounds gave her an eerie feeling and her thoughts drifted back to the young couple who had never had a chance to live in their dream house. She didn't believe in ghosts, yet, at times, it had seemed to her that she felt the presence of the young ones, as if their spirits filled the rooms. But now they must be happy, she thought, because they must be aware that no people could ever love this place more than the Omars. Just the same, she wished that she could stop thinking of Judy and Tom. If she told Ernest about her feelings, he would just laugh at her. But this morning, now when the sun cast its first rays through the window, she was almost sure she heard them depart, as if a door had opened softly, and then closed with a quiet click. Barbara was almost tempted to get out of bed to look out through the window, but she forced herself to lie still. How silly it would be to think she could hear, much less see ghosts. Now she must rid her mind of such inane thoughts.

She was glad when Ernest moved.

"Are you awake?" she asked.

"Yes, wide awake and thankful for that. I have had the most horrible dreams all night. I'm glad the night is over."

"Did you dream about the hospital? That you were operating? You must miss it all, Ern. You were so close to everything there for so many years."

"At times, Barbara, I do miss my practice, and I wonder if I did the right thing. But then when I wander around our acre and sit in the sun and relax and smell good things cooking in the kitchen and see my wife sitting by the wishing well, then, Barb, I'm glad that the rushing is over and that we all can enjoy this beautiful spot on God's earth. There is only one gloomy note—that's Gail. She is certainly not happy and she's not close to us as she once was. Ever since the night we told her she was not going to college, she has been like a lost child."

"I've been doing a lot of thinking, too. I wonder if we did the right thing. We can't take her out of the world. As she said, it's the only world she knows and wants. I have changed my mind, Ern. I feel now that we must let her go to college with her friends. Her whole personality is changing and I'm really worried about her."

"I had almost changed my mind too, Barb. Do you think there is still a chance that she could enter with the freshman class at Skidmore?"

"I know she can. I called the college and inquired. There are two openings so if we make up our minds and let the registrar know right away, Gail can get in. Let's do it, Ern. She will be so happy."

The bedroom was silent for a moment. The sun was rising now and everywhere there was a golden glow. Barbara waited; everything had gone so much smoother than she had expected. She felt that Ernest had come to the same conclusion and that was a welcome surprise.

Then Ernest spoke.

"We will tell Gail this morning," he said softly.

"Oh, Ern, I'm so happy! This is the right thing to do and now we will all be happy."

Barbara snuggled close to her husband and felt secure in his embrace. All was going to be right again. Why had she worried so about it?

"This calls for a celebration," suggested Ernest. "How would Mrs. Omar like to make some popovers for breakfast since that's our daughter's favorite?"

"Of course, I'll make popovers, but you have to help beat the batter. You know I like to use my old-fashioned egg beater and you know how long it takes to get them right."

"Agreed!"

While they were dressing, Barbara was regretful. Why

had they waited so long? Why had they wasted a whole summer? But Ernest had been so tired and discouraged with all the sickness, crime, pollution, and moral decay that he had gotten her into the same mood and then they had taken out their frustration on Gail. But Gail would understand that, too. She would forgive them and be happy.

It had been a long time since Barbara had made popovers, and she had forgotten that they took almost an hour to bake. But she and Ernest worked together and set the table on the porch and Barbara had even picked some baby zinnias for a centerpiece. When the bacon had been fried and the eggs scrambled, and the popovers were just ready to take from the oven, Ernest ran up the stairs to get Gail.

"Tell her to come in her robe," said Barbara. "You know popovers can't wait."

Barbara was just placing the popovers in the breadbasket when Ernest slowly descended the stairs. He had a note in his hand.

"Our daughter has flown the coop," he laughed. "Here is a note saying that she has climbed the mountain this morning. You know, I think she has really begun to love our surroundings. This is the first time she has gone off climbing the hills in the early morning. I'll bet she's having breakfast with the Briggses."

"And what are we going to do with all these popovers? They really came out just right. What a shame that she should have picked this morning to go mountain climbing."

"I'll make up for her! I promise I'll eat six of them!"

"And I will eat the other six—maybe. That really is quite a bit, but this mountain air makes me hungry."

In spite of their disappointment that Gail was not with

them for this special breakfast, the Omars were light-hearted. Later Barbara went with Ernest to fish in the small rowboat, having made one condition—that her husband bait her hooks. The fish were biting and Barbara caught a small bass, while Ernest pulled in several perch. Nothing could have tasted better for lunch than freshly caught fish from their own lake. They ate at the picnic table by the wishing well. Ernest Omar was in the best mood Barbara had seen him in for some weeks.

He was glad now, she thought, that they were doing the right thing by Gail. It had been a burden for him, too. If only she had known! They could all have been really happy in the months past.

After lunch Barbara and Ernest began to wonder about Gail. Why was she gone so long? It was not like Gail to stay with the Briggses most of the day. She had not said *where* she was climbing, and something might have happened to her.

"Gail should not go off alone like this," said Ernest. "Even though this place seems free from danger, one never knows. From now on we must tell her not to go up the mountain alone."

Barbara laughed. "I'm sure she is up at the Briggses. You know how they love company. I'm sure they have kept her talking. But I think we should drive up the hill and fetch her."

Ernest agreed and soon they were on their way up the steep hill to their nearest neighbors. They found Mrs. Briggs out in her flower garden. She greeted them warmly.

"We have come for our daughter," smiled Barbara. "I'm afraid she is overstaying her welcome."

Mrs. Briggs looked puzzled for a moment, then her face broke into an understanding smile. This must be the moment Gail had told her about. She had better not let them know that the package had not been left there today.

"Gail is not here now," she said sweetly, "but she left something behind her with strict orders to give it to her mother the moment you came asking for her. Wait just a second, I'll be right back."

Mrs. Briggs returned with the gaily wrapped package and handed it to Barbara.

"I know this isn't a birthday, but whatever day it is, I wish you happiness."

Barbara looked dumbfounded.

"Whatever day it is, Gail has made it a special day. How long has it been since she left here?"

Mrs. Briggs shook her head.

"I am not accustomed to these intrigues and I don't want to be caught in a lie. Your daughter left this with me several days ago. She said that one day her mom and dad would come driving up the hill asking for her and that was the day I was to give you the gift."

"I'd better open it then," said Barbara with a bit of alarm in her voice. If this was a mystery to Mrs. Briggs, it was even more of a puzzle to her. And where was Gail?

Barbara untied the ribbon and slowly unwrapped the box. She lifted the lid and looked into the box at the letter. But she did not take it out. Already she had glanced at some of the words. She forced a smile.

"It's just a joke, I guess. That girl! What she can't think up!"

But Barbara's face was white and strained and she could feel Ernest peering searchingly at her.

"We'd better drive home now, Ernest. Thank you, Mrs. Briggs, for putting up with Gail. She loves to play jokes."

"I don't mind at all! But she seemed very serious about this." She smiled at Barbara. "If I had my girl back, she could play a joke on me every day. Don't be in such a hurry though. Wait until I can get you some tomatoes from the garden."

They waited while Mrs. Briggs disappeared again. Barbara did not speak and Ernest questioned only with his eyes. A heavy silence fell over the mountainside.

Mrs. Briggs appeared with a bag of ripe red tomatoes.

"I don't think we ever have had any tomatoes as big or as red and juicy as these," she chattered.

"They're beautiful," said Dr. Omar. "I know they are going to be delicious. Thanks so very much." And he started up the motor.

Barbara called her thanks from the car. She was impatient to read the note completely, and after they had waved to Mrs. Briggs and started down the hill, Barbara began to read the letter's contents to her husband, the tears brimming from her eyes. When she had finished, she hugged the paper to her heart.

"How could she do this to us, Ern?" she sobbed. "How could she run away and do it in such a way that we couldn't find her? I know now when she left. It must have been the noise I heard just at daybreak. I wonder where she went and where she is just now?"

"Crying is not going to help, Barb. We were too late with our understanding, but I never would have thought that she could do something like this."

"We have to do something!" Barbara tried to hold back her tears. "If only we knew where she is! But it had to come, Ern. I knew it would. Deep down in my heart I knew something would happen, and this is only the beginning. It is the curse on our house. It has even reached us."

"Don't be silly, honey! You know very well there is no curse. It is us, you and me. Gail was lonely without her friends and we thought it would be enough for her just to have her family. But we will find her . . . I think she will come back soon, you wait and see. Gail is not used to being away from home and earning a living. What in the world would she do?"

Barbara was reading the letter over again and the tears kept coming. Suddenly the house down in the valley looked lonely. She felt chilly although the afternoon was warm. There must be something they could do. Then she remembered Fran Sawyer. She was Gail's best friend. She must telephone Fran. Surely Fran could tell her something that would make it easier to find Gail.

Barbara called Fran as soon as she got home. In a choked voice she told Fran the story, but Fran was evasive, which made Barbara even more convinced that she knew something. It was only when Barbara began to tell Fran that they had changed their minds and were now willing for Gail to attend Skidmore that Fran began to loosen up.

"It is so important, Fran, that we find her because Skidmore has to know very soon. There is a deadline, and we know that is where she wants to go."

"If she had known that she could have gone, Gail never would have run away," said Fran. "I think I can talk now without breaking a confidence. She is going to California."

"To California!"

"Yes! Lynn moved there, you know. Gail is going to contact Lynn who plans to help her get work. Don't worry, Mrs. Omar, as soon as Gail hears she can go to Skidmore, she will be right home, and now *I* am the happiest person on earth. Now Gail and I can be there together. I just dreaded the thought of going without Gail. We were always so close, you know."

"Bless you," said Barbara. "Bless you for being such a good friend, and bless you for telling me. I can sleep now and tomorrow or the next day we will get hold of Gail in California. I shall call Lynn's folks. But first we must give Gail time to get there."

Barbara could smile again! Gail would return as soon as she heard the glad news.

But still Ernest and Barbara ate dinner in silence. Later they took a walk down the country road. This was the same road their daughter had taken in the morning, starting out alone for the nearest town, miles away.

Oh, Gail, Barbara was thinking, you think you are so grown up, but you are still a little girl and you do still need us, as much as we need you.

"Now let's chase the gloom away," said Ernest, as they returned to the house. "We must believe that all will be well, very soon."

"And I shall pray that God sends down His angels to be with Gail wherever she is. She will be safe . . . I must know that she will be safe."

It was not easy for the Omars to go to sleep that night, although Ernest dropped off first. Finally, even Barbara's tired eyes closed, and rest came to the troubled mother —she need think no more tonight.

Outside the house a full August moon shone over Golden Acre. The trees stood as silent sentinels and the birds had long ago tucked their heads under their wings. Even the loons on the lake had anchored for the night. All nature was at peace. Soon a new day would dawn and all of God's beautiful world would begin to stir again.

But the two sleeping parents in the yellow house below the sheltering mountains would awaken wiser. They had learned a sad lesson that they would not soon forget. No matter how dear is your child to your heart, you cannot force that young life into a mold of your design. If you try, something fragile, beautiful, and rare will disappear.

The young must be free to try their own wings. They must be allowed to soar and even fall, only to soar again. They must be released from the security of the nest, to flutter and then surge, as they seek their own heart's desire—for find it they will.

8

Those first days in Earthend, Pennsylvania, went by faster than any others in Gail's memory. Her life was filled to overflowing with little tasks she would never have dreamt she would perform. But it was a joy to do them, because she was doing them for Doug and helping him in his work with the church. Gail could not explain what had happened to her, but this young preacher had become the focus of her whole life. She knew only that she wanted to be wherever Doug was, even if it meant this forsaken little mountain town. He must feel something, too, she thought, although he had never expressed it in words. There was that mutual understanding between them. She sensed that he was glad when they were together and their conversations flowed easily, sprinkled with comradely fun and laughter.

And Gail had found a faithful friend in Helen Armstrong, even though the plump woman was well beyond middle age. There was a kinship between them, and Mrs. Armstrong's happy laughter and lighthearted manner were a tonic for Gail's soul. She would never forget the

day she and Doug had arrived in Earthend, and Mrs.
Armstrong had fairly run out of the church to greet the
new pastor.

"I am Mrs. Armstrong, a member of the pulpit commit-
tee," she had said with a smile, reaching out her hand.
"Welcome to our town, Pastor Rhodes!" And before Doug
had time to reply, she had continued. "I'm so pleased to
see that you are *two*. That was the only drawback when
we were voting to call you. You see, our parsonage needs
a woman. It is too large for a man to live there alone. Well,
pastor, you have seen the size of it."

Gail had noticed Doug blush and her heart had begun
to pound. Already people were drawing conclusions, and
now Doug would be put on the spot because of her. But it
only took him a moment to regain his composure. He had
grinned and shaken the outstretched hand.

"Mrs. Armstrong, let me introduce Miss Gail Olsen.
She is not going to live in the parsonage with me; she is
just a friend who decided, on the spur of the moment, to
accompany me. There was no time to consult you. I
learned that Gail was looking for a place to volunteer her
services, and I felt we could use her. If not, she will be on
her way back. I know it isn't up to me alone, so I'll leave it
in your hands. I am sorry to disappoint you about the
parsonage."

"Oh, that! Never mind! I am always speaking out of
turn. I'm glad you came along, Miss Olsen. Welcome to
you, too."

"Just call me Gail," she had said as she returned Mrs.
Armstrong's firm handshake. "I hope I won't be any trouble, but I have to find a place to live if I am to stay on
here."

"That part is easily settled," beamed Mrs. Armstrong.
"You see, I live in a big house, too, almost as large as the
parsonage and I have been alone since my dear husband

graduated to eternity a year ago. I can guarantee that the church will be grateful for your service. We will be very pleased to have you work for us, and if you can give of your time so generously to the Lord, I certainly can offer you room and board as my part of the gift—that is, of course, if you'd like to live with me."

Gail had been overwhelmed by such kindness.

"Thank you, Mrs. Armstrong. I'm so grateful for your kind offer. I'm sure I will love your house and I'll try not to be too much bother."

"Oh, we'll get along just fine! It will be fun to have a pretty young friend in my home. But now you must excuse me. I have to telephone our moderator, Mr. Morrison, who is expecting you for dinner and tell him that you are two instead of one."

"And, in the meantime, I will show Gail the church," offered Doug.

"Please do! I'll be with you in a minute."

Gail walked with Doug into the tiny building, and they stopped in the foyer and looked into the sanctuary. It was a simple, modest church, but even in its plainness, warm and appealing.

"I like it, Doug—your church. It feels good—so comforting and warm. I can't wait to hear you preach from that high pulpit."

Doug looked thoughtful as his eyes focused on the pulpit.

"At times, being a minister scares me . . . the sacredness of it and the challenge to relay the Word of God to people each Sunday morning. I almost wish the pulpit were lower. I feel so unworthy for such a noble task, but I hope to be a good preacher."

"You will be, Doug! I have a feeling that you will be terrific! And with me as your helper, how can you fail? We should be able to move the whole town."

There was no time for an answer because Mrs. Armstrong appeared in the doorway. It was time to move on.

Dinner at the Morrisons had been delicious. Their house was warm and comfortable and they were gay, friendly people. They had accepted Gail without question and thanked her for coming along. Doug had seemed pleased, and it appeared that everything was working out well.

After Gail had gone to Mrs. Armstrong's that night and had been settled in a large room facing the mountains, she could not believe that it had been only this morning that she had left Golden Acre. She could hardly believe all the things that had taken place. In spite of a twinge of loneliness for home, she would not change what had happened, and if there were now a choice between Earthend and Skidmore, Gail felt it would be Earthend she would choose. Sleep did not come easily as she wondered about Mom and Dad and how they would worry about her. She had done a cruel thing after they had given her so much love and security. And Lynn, what would she think when Gail never arrived in California? She would think something had happened to Gail and contact Fran. Still, she could not send them a letter revealing her whereabouts. How would she ever be able to untangle the mess she had made? If only they, all of them, could know she was well taken care of and living, though not in luxury, in Helen Armstrong's warm, pleasant home and with a good-looking preacher keeping an eye on her. It was kind of the congregation to accept her so readily and to give her a job, even if it was without a salary.

The next morning Gail sat in front of the large desk in the church office with her new boss facing her.

"I'm scared!" she confessed. "You know, Doug, I have never been a secretary before."

Doug looked serious.

"The job is not going to be what you may have anticipated, Gail. I have my own idea of church work, and now I
can put it to the test. There are different ways to build up a
church, and both of us must work at it. I believe in personal contact and that is where you are going to help me.
You will not be sitting at a desk, typing. You will be out in
the town winning people for God."

Gail's eyes opened wide!

"You can't mean that I'm going to preach to people,
Doug. I could never do that, no matter how much I
wanted to help."

"No, my dear, I assure you there will be no preaching,
just a lot of talking—and walking! I want you to call on
people, to go from door to door, ringing doorbells, just
like a political campaigner. The church attendance is
very low, I have learned, and I want you just to be yourself. Smile and win their hearts as you invite them to
come on Sunday morning to hear the new preacher and
give him a good start."

"I hope I can do it," gasped Gail. "I'm not a very
outgoing person, but I'll do my best."

"That's all I ask, so go to it."

Gail had not been very happy, at first, about her job.
This was a task that would take tact and persuasion. She
would have to sell herself before she could sell the
church, but she started out bravely and the first day she
covered twenty-five houses. It hadn't been bad at all. Gail
found the people friendly and courteous. Most of them
invited her in; some even offered her a cup of coffee or a
look at the family pictures. By the end of the day, she had
her introduction speech down pat and her smile felt
glued to her face.

"I am Gail Olsen," she had said. "I represent Pastor

Rhodes, the new minister. He's a terrific speaker and I am inviting you to come and listen to him this Sunday morning. We'd like the church full that first time, to encourage him, and we need your cooperation."

She found she was really making contact with the people, and her heart was light when she returned to the church office.

"Now if only they come as they have promised, I'll feel that your idea is working," she told Doug.

"Even if they don't come, you've done a good job, Gail, and I'm proud of you. I think you're going to be just what I need to get started. And one thing you have proven, that you're willing to try anything. It will be rewarding, you'll see. There are still three more days until Sunday."

And Doug was right. Gail did feel rewarded when she entered the sanctuary that first Sunday morning and saw every seat in the church filled. Doug seemed to have found the key to Earthend's church problems right at the start.

Gail was as excited as if it were her church, too, when she saw Doug walking up the aisle behind the choir. He looked more handsome than ever in his black robe and her heart beat a little faster. Someday . . . could she hope to be his wife? That was all she would ask of life —and of God (if He would hear her prayers after the way she had lied). Anyway she would try to make up for it by working twice as hard at anything she was asked to do. If only she could tell Doug, if only he would understand and not condemn her for running away from home and using an assumed name. But Gail was afraid that the first thing he would do would be to contact her parents and have her shipped right back to Golden Acre, and she could not take that chance.

Soon she lost herself in the worship service. The choir had sung an anthem and their untrained voices sent a simple yet harmonious tribute to God. Then Doug began his sermon and an expectant hush fell over the congregation.

"I am happy this morning," Doug began, "to see the church filled. This is the greatest welcome you could have given me. I am glad to be here with you. And I haven't come to give you any fancy speeches or rules of living. I have come only to share with you the Word of God. I plan to preach right from the Book . . . God's Book. My own grandfather introduced it to me as a map for the journey from earth to heaven, and as I have followed this map, I have always found the right road. When I have a decision to make, I consult the Book and get the answer there. The guide is there, even for the modern times we live in. So many different sources are giving us directions as to what is right or wrong, but if you follow God's Word, you don't have to be confused. The way is plainly marked.

"It's all summed up in the Ten Commandments and the Sermon on the Mount. From these directions we can trim up our lives. We must be especially alert to the little foxes that spoil the vineyard. If dishonesty creeps in, we must catch it and get rid of it right then. It's easy to excuse a white lie, but there are no white lies in God's Book. To live by His Word we have to be totally honest, even in the smallest things, honest with ourselves and with our God. . . ."

Doug was an excellent speaker. Surely he could have had a large church, Gail was thinking, but he acted as if this church were the most important in the world. Here he was giving of himself to these country people—his only aim to get them all to live by God's Book. She was sure God would bless his efforts. But what would he think if he knew that his secretary lived a lie—she couldn't bear to think of that! Doug couldn't stand dishonesty; he had made that very clear this morning.

The worship service had been a success and Mrs. Armstrong was beaming from ear to ear as they returned to her home that morning. Doug was with them, too. She had given a blanket invitation to him to take all his Sunday dinners at her home.

"Gail and I would love to have the preacher for dinner on Sundays," she had said. "It will give us something to look forward to all week."

And Doug had accepted.

"You are so kind, Mrs. Armstrong, and you can be my family, until I get one of my own. Thank you so much."

Doug was pleased with his first Sunday, too.

"I hope they will all be back next Sunday," he had said to Gail while they sat in the living room waiting for the roast to finish cooking.

"Do I have to call all this week, too?" she asked.

"Yes, I think you should keep on until you have contacted every family in the town."

"That could take a year!"

"Well, I hope you'll stay that long."

Gail laughed. "I will if you don't fire me first."

"I won't if you keep on the way you have started. And to prove how pleased I am with your help, I'll give you Monday off. You see, that's my day off, too. And since we both have the same day off, would Miss Olsen consider spending tomorrow with me? I'd like to drive around the mountain—in fact, I'd like to see what is on the other side."

"I'd really like that," said Gail.

"I'll pick you up at ten tomorrow morning."

Mrs. Armstrong was thrilled when Gail shared her happiness after Doug had gone.

"I'd like to see you two together," Helen had said. "In fact, I'm already picturing you in the parsonage. The two of you are so right for each other."

Gail looked seriously into her friend's face.

"Do you really mean that, Helen? I would like nothing better. I'm very, very fond of Doug, but I don't think he has ever thought of me as anything more than a friend."

"Perhaps you have known each other too long?"

"No, not that long. He comes from Vermont and I, from New Hampshire. I have only known Doug a short time."

"And your parents, Gail? What do they think of Doug? I've never asked anything about you. I sort of hoped that you would volunteer some information, since I don't like to pry."

"I don't want to talk about my parents. It's just one of those things. I feel as if I come from nowhere. Someday, though, I might be able to open up and tell you all about myself. Will you be patient and wait until I can?"

"Of course," smiled Helen Armstrong. "I know you for what you are, and you are already very dear to me. But if you ever need to talk, remember I'm always here."

"Thank you. I'm so grateful and right now I think of you as my closest friend. I know I can trust you."

Gail was smiling, but there was an ache in her heart. How much she wanted to tell Helen about Mom and Dad and Golden Acre, but she didn't know just how much she dared trust anyone. No one must know that she had run away and was now hiding from her family. Not yet anyway.

Monday morning came with glorious sunshine and a cloudless blue sky. Doug drove up right at ten, and Gail was eagerly waiting. Helen waved at them as they drove off.

It was a perfect day and their laughter and conversation seemed to increase with their hours together. Hamburgers and Coke was lunch in a run-down wayside stand at the base of the mountain.

"So this is what is on the other side," teased Gail.

"We shall find a place more gracious for our dinner, even if I have to drive all the way to Pittsburgh," laughed Doug.

When afternoon arrived, they found themselves in a small town with a variety of stores and Gail asked if Doug minded being left alone while she did some shopping.

"I need some clothes in the worst way," she confessed, and she needed money, too. She wanted to cash some traveler's checks while she was away from Earthend since those checks bore the name of Gail Omar. By dinner time she had found a bank and cashed a good many checks and had done some shopping. She felt especially gay since the day seemed to be going so well. Doug had hunted for the right place to eat—a lovely restaurant overlooking a river—and the food was delicious.

"You *did* find a great place," said Gail.

"And we're not too far from Pittsburgh either, I want you to know. We have a long trip home."

But to Gail there was no way too long when she was with Doug. She only wished the day would go on forever.

After dinner, as they were driving along, Doug suddenly became serious.

"How about letting me have just a glimpse of your past, Gail? You know I think a lot of you, and I should know something about you."

"Oh, don't spoil our perfect day, Doug! Honestly, it would make me very unhappy if I had to think back. Just now I want to live for each new day. You tell me more about yourself instead; you always have happy stories."

"I have unhappy ones too, Gail. Everyone has both sad and glad memories. I'll tell you one of my not-so-happy ones, just so you will know."

"Not too sad, I hope."

"Even if it were, it happened a long time ago."

"Are you going to give me a little sermonette?"

"You could call it that . . . it's the story of a dog—a dog named Jeff. He, too, came from nowhere."

I think I was about ten years old and Grandma and Gramp let me run free in the woods near their home. I loved to find new trails and follow them to their end. And so, on an autumn day when I was tramping through the woods, feeling the dry leaves under my shoes, I heard a whimper—like a low moan. Guided by the sound, I came to a dog, dirty, unkempt, and bleeding from several wounds. He was lying on a pile of leaves and he looked so pitiful that my heart broke into little pieces. I knew I had to bring him home, but he was too heavy for me to pick up and carry, and he was too weak to walk. So I gathered all my little-boy strength and little by little, I managed to drag him home. He seemed to know I was trying to help.

When we got home, Grandma gave him some warm milk and we bathed him and cleaned his wounds. When Gramp came home, he gave him a shot of something, but he said there was very little chance that the dog would pull through. Our foundling slept on a quilt in a corner of the kitchen that night, and even though I knew Grandma was not too fond of dogs, she was wonderful to Jeff, which was the name I had given him. By the next morning he was much improved, and in a couple of weeks we discovered what a beautiful collie he was—so friendly and alert. I had nursed him back to life. He must have been in the woods for days before I found him and he would probably have died had I not come upon him. Gramp said it looked as if some wild animal had attacked him. He had no tags or identification, and soon he was truly *my* dog. We romped through the woods together; he was my pal and slept by my bed at night. Those were some of the happiest weeks of my childhood. Then one day, as we were walking down the road, a car pulled up beside us and a man spoke to me.

"Hey, boy," he said, "where did you get that dog?"

"I found him in the woods a few weeks ago. He was hurt and I took him home and nursed him. He's *my* dog!"

"No, he's not!" said a boy about my age, from the back seat. "He is *my* Trent. Someone stole him. He must have run away from the thief and gotten lost in the woods. Maybe some animal hurt him. Trent is a gentle dog."

The boy got out of the car and Jeff bounded up to him, licking his face. It was all too much for me.

"Jeff," I called. "Come here, Jeff!"

He came with his head down and his tail wasn't wagging. I patted his head.

"Jeff," I said softly, "you are mine, aren't you?"

He licked my hand as if to tell me that he loved me too, but his eyes were on the other boy.

"Little man," said the boy's father, "we are so grateful to you for saving Trent's life. We love him very much. Ever since he disappeared, we have been driving and looking down one road after another, advertising in newspapers and on the radio, trying to find him. We had almost given up."

I stood there paralyzed—I was cold all over.

"Okay, Jeff," I said. "You can go if you want to."

Jeff looked at me once more, then ran to the boy, and I never saw a happier reunion. The boy took him into the car and I just stood there. No matter how I tried, I couldn't stop the tears from rolling down my cheeks.

The man reached out his hand, and I gave him mine. "I'm sorry," he said, "to take him away from you, but I know you understand. Here, let me give you some money for all your trouble."

"No thank you, sir," I replied."I could never take money for taking care of Jeff. I'm happy for the time I had him."

"You are a fine boy," said the man.

I tried to smile. "I'm glad he is happy to be back with you."

I turned and began to walk toward home. I heard the car drive off and Jeff's happy woofs came through the open window. I cried all the way home. Grandma found me sitting on the back steps, my head in my hands, sobbing my heart out. She took me in her arms, but nothing would console me. Gramp said he was proud of me, that I was a real man. That made me feel a little taller, but the hurt lingered for weeks and weeks. I missed Jeff so much. It still hurts to think about him. But it was a great lesson in life. That's the end of the sermonette, Gail.

"That was a very sad, but touching story, Doug. Thanks for sharing it with me."

Doug took Gail's hand in his and looked at her tenderly.

"You see, you remind me a little of Jeff. I found you as I found him. He was bleeding on the outside—I think perhaps your wounds are inside. Jeff had run away, or been taken away from home and was hurt and alone. I don't know your situation, but I won't let myself become too fond of you, because you belong somewhere else. For a time I thought Jeff was mine because I had found him in the woods. I never thought of him as coming from somewhere where he had been loved and sheltered. Someone might come for you, too, to claim you because they have been looking for you as those people were looking for Jeff. I shall never let myself go through an agony like that again . . . I know you belong somewhere."

Gail didn't answer. She was too close to crying. She only squeezed his hand hard and inched a little closer to his side of the car. He had said so much in so few words, but she lacked the courage to explain. If only she could be sure he would understand and not send her away! But she could not risk that because she loved him too much to lose him.

They didn't talk much during the last part of the ride. Each seemed lost in his own throughts, and when they drove up in front of Mrs. Armstrong's house, Doug walked her impersonally to the door and said good-night.

"It has been a good day, Gail. Thank you for spending it with me. In the morning we'll plan your calling for the week, and I'll see you at nine o'clock sharp."

Gail opened the door and walked into Mrs. Armstrong's living room. She heard the car drive off and her heart went with him. She had so hoped he would take her in his arms and kiss her. Perhaps he never would, although he had certainly hinted that he cared for her. Now she was more mixed up than ever. Gail was glad that Helen was asleep. She just could not have faced her friend tonight. If she had been there to greet her, Gail might have told Mrs. Armstrong everything, because she felt so lost and alone and confused.

9

There *is* a curse on that house!" moaned Mrs. Briggs. "I knew this would happen. I am sorry now that we let you buy the place. We should have burned the house to the ground. I feel responsible for fine people like you being caught in a trap like this."

Barbara Omar looked into Mrs. Briggs's sad eyes from which she was trying to blink back tears.

"We don't believe in the story of the curse—you know that, Mrs. Briggs. It is neither the house, nor you who sold it to us, that is to blame. Please don't even talk like that. The fault belongs to my husband and me. We denied Gail her chance to go to college. We tried to take her out of the mad world and thought that Golden Acre would be a peaceful sanctuary for her, too. We meant well, but we were wrong."

"I just can't believe that a girl as intelligent and fine as Gail would run away from a wonderful home like yours. The whole thing just doesn't make sense."

"Young people can do almost anything when they feel trapped, and I'm sure that is the way our daughter felt.

The young need to be guided but at the same time they must have some freedom to try their own strength. They can't be forced to follow someone else's way. Oh, we were so wrong!"

"I wish I could help you, Mrs. Omar. If only I could tell you something that would give you a clue. But I only know that when she visited us she was as happy as a lark. She said that one day you would come driving up the hill asking for her, and then I was to surrender the package which she left."

"It was clever of her to think of that. She knew that by the time we would start looking for her, she would be far away. My only hope has been that her best friend, Fran Sawyer, in whom Gail always confided, was right, that Gail was going to California to meet another friend. But so far, Gail has not arrived there. There is no trace of her. We have contacted the police—we have advertised for her and published her picture in newspapers across the country. Doctor Omar even went on television to plead with her to come home. But no one has been able to find her. We are so afraid that something awful has happened to her."

"That is the curse!" insisted Mrs. Briggs. "The first part might be your fault, but Gail's being swallowed up by the earth, *that* is the bad omen, the tragic spell that hangs over Judy's and Tom's house."

"No, my dear! No! No! That can't be so. We shall find her. We can't live without her. She is our only child."

"I know," said Mrs. Briggs, her voice filled with sorrow. "I know how you feel. I had an only child, too. She was as loving and sweet and beautiful as your Gail. I felt the same way when we lost our Judy. You think you can't go on, but you do. You just go on, day by day, week by week, and year by year. But you never stop hurting and you never forget. At least *you* can hope."

The two mothers sat in silence for a while on the porch which overlooked the valley. It was afternoon on that September day, and the birds trilled merrily in the trees. The sun showered the mountainside beauty with purest gold. But the two women were untouched by the lovely scene. They were tied by a common bond; they each mourned the loss of a daughter, which blinded them to the panoramic view. Mrs. Briggs thought of her Judy who slept in the small cemetery at the foot of the mountain, and Mrs. Omar thought of her Gail, who had disappeared. While fearing the worst, Barbara was still clinging to the hope that she would find her lost child. Finally she arose.

"I must drive home. Ernest is waiting down at Golden Acre. The strain is beginning to age him. It hurts to see how he has grayed considerably just in these past weeks since Gail left. I will see you again soon. Please come down and see us often. We get so lonesome these days."

"We will and I shall pray for Gail every night."

Mrs. Briggs walked Barbara to the car.

"Do drive carefully down the hill," she warned.

Barbara waved from the car. "Don't worry. I almost crawl down that mountain road."

As Barbara drove into her driveway, she saw her husband sitting on the green bench by the lake. She parked the car and walked over and sat beside him.

"It's been good for me to talk to Mrs. Briggs, but she can't give us any clue at all. She is heartbroken and feels so guilty. She's convinced that the curse from this house has now fallen on us. She almost makes me believe it, too, but I would never let her know that. She has a heavy enough burden to bear."

"While you were gone, I have been sitting here thinking," said Dr. Omar, taking Barbara's hand in his. "I have been remembering happier times—when I first saw Gail there in the hospital and those early years of her childhood and then the school times. What a dear child she was—always so full of fun and laughter—until the day I told her that she couldn't go to college. How could I have been so stupid? Now I would give anything, do anything just to see her once more."

Barbara didn't answer. Her own heart was too full of sorrow. She just squeezed Ernest's hand tightly. It was time to prepare dinner, even if meals seemed to have lost their flavor. Still, they had to eat to keep going. Each night they telephoned Fran, but there was never any news. Tonight would be the last night Fran would be in Lexington, as the next day she would leave for Skidmore. Fran was as worried as they were, and she felt it was partly her fault for suggesting that Gail leave home. Lynn, too, felt partly to blame, as she had shared in the plans.

"Somehow we have to keep living without her, Ern," said Barbara the next morning, "but we mustn't leave this place to take those trips we planned. We must always be here in case Gail should call. Winter will come, and then we will be snowed in here in this wilderness. Just you and I will sit here and it will be a lonely winter. Somehow Golden Acre has lost its charm for me as I think of the lonely days head."

"Still we have to be grateful that we have each other, Barb, and not despair. Someday we'll find Gail. At times I wonder if it is me who is being punished for giving up surgery when there is such a need for skilled doctors. The thought haunts me. So many people need help. Was I selfish to retire? I do miss the hospital and my colleagues and my practice. And you, Barb, must miss your friends, the luncheons, the shopping in big stores, and the theater parties, not to mention our dinners with my associates. But most of all, we both miss Gail's happy laughter. I would turn the clock back and not change a thing if we only had Gail home again."

But the days were gloomy. Barbara cried often, and Ernest tried to busy himself with outside work.

When Ernest drove into the city now, Barbara stayed home, hoping for some news of Gail. Someone always was there—waiting.

One day when Ernest returned from a trip to Boston, he brought a present for Barbara, an eight-month-old German Shepherd puppy. She was black and tan, with a star on her forehead, and Barbara was delighted.

"I shall call her Lady," she said, patting the soft hair. "Now I'll have someone to go with me on walks and to keep me company when you are away, Ern. You could not have given me a dearer present. She'll not fill Gail's place, but she will be a great help."

Soon they had said farewell to September, and October arrived with its frosty nights, turning the woodland into an enchanted forest. The trees, garbed in autumn scarlet, gold, and russet brown, were even now beginning to shed their foliage, and as the leaves floated dreamily to the forest floor they bore a wistful reminder of the fading summer and the lonely winter to come. The bright hues had disappeared—frost had faded the mums, and the rosy MacIntosh in the apple orchard were ready to be harvested and stored. The most brightly colored birds had flown southward and the V formations of migrating geese were a familiar pattern against the sky. Soon the scattered pinecones would be blanketed with snow—and all would be still in the forest. Darkness fell early, but the crackling fire kindled to dispel the evening chill did little to warm the Omar's hearts.

For, almost two months had passed without a word from Gail. Barbara and Ernest had all but accepted the fact that they might never hear from her again, but agreed that if they must face life without her, they must be brave and not let themselves break under the sorrow.

One night Barbara had retired early to read, leaving Ernest to watch one of his favorite television programs. As she lay in bed, she slid her hand gently over her left breast. She had done this several times before, each time refusing to dwell on the fear that gripped her. There was a hard swelling there, but it was very small—no bigger than a marble. But tonight she tried to face the possible situation. Whatever was there had grown larger and harder and was sore when she pressed it. Barbara sat up in bed. There must be an infection of some kind in her breast. Of course, that was all it was. Or maybe she had bumped herself without realizing it. She must not panic.

"I will wait one more week and see if the lump has changed," she told herself. "Then if it is still there, I will have Ernest look at it."

She tried to interest herself in the book she was reading, but found she had lost track of the plot. If only there were someone besides Ern with whom she could discuss this, someone who would assure her that all was well. Perhaps she had even brought this upon herself, because of her unhappiness over Gail's disappearance. She could talk things over with Mrs. Briggs, but she would probably just tell her that this was more evidence of the curse that was on the house in which they lived. More and more dreadful things would happen, Mrs. Briggs would say, and as she thought about it, Barbara almost believed it. Maybe she was being punished for not showing more understanding of Gail's needs. . . . Still, she would wait another week and check again.

Barbara tried to be especially tender and sweet to Ernest. She wanted so badly to make up for Gail's absence in some small way. They look long rides together, and nature was so breathtakingly beautiful that Barbara could hardly believe that the scenery was real. They dined in picturesque eating places and shopped in antique shops and boutiques, now empty of tourists. Each day they tried to fill with new pleasures and entertainment. Barbara had given up the idea of sitting home, waiting for Gail's call. She had resigned herself halfheartedly to the realization that the call would never come. She tried not to think of the next time she would examine herself. Barbara hoped with every fiber of her being that the next time she felt for the lump it would be gone.

Fran was enrolled and settled at Skidmore now and Barbara had a letter from her almost every week.

"Gail would have loved this place," Fran wrote. "If she were only here, we would have such fun together. I will not enjoy myself completely until I hear from her, and I hope it is soon."

Fran's letters were very dear to Barbara and Ernest. She was a darling, and Barbara understood now why she and Gail had been so close.

And Lady was growing, too—Barbara loved her more each day. She even proved herself to be quite a watchdog. If anyone approached the house, she would bark with such fury that the person hesitated before coming up to the front door. Yes, Lady stood guard. Barbara wondered what would happen if Gail came up the walk. Would Lady sense that she was part of the family and treat her as such? Oh, if only that day would come! But never had Barbara known that a dog could be such a friend. At night Lady nuzzled very close to Barbara's chair in the living room and sometimes she put her cold nose in Barbara's lap as a sign of devotion.

The Briggses came down to visit often now. They never mentioned the curse since Ernest had made a point of asking them not to.

"It only makes it harder for us," he had explained. "I shall never believe in such superstition no matter how many things go wrong for us. So let's not speak of it again. Barbara and I would appreciate it."

And the Briggses never had.

Ernest busied himself by chopping firewood. They would need quite a stack for the winter. And Barbara picked pinecones in the woods for kindling while Lady romped beside her. There was only an artificial contentment, but it made the days pass a little more quickly.

Then a week had passed and Barbara retired early as before. But even before she touched her breast she knew what she would find. The lump was larger than even she had feared. She had been living in a fool's paradise. No matter how much she hated to worry Ernest, she knew that she would have to tell him. Drops of sweat broke out on Barbara's forehead and a penetrating fear gripped her.

"Dear God," she prayed, "don't let anything like that happen to me."

She couldn't make herself put it into medical terms. Her heart ached as she searched for the words which would not alarm Ernest too much.

Suddenly Barbara looked up, and there he stood in the doorway, smiling at her.

"You aren't reading," he said.

"No, dear. I can't read tonight. Something is wrong, Ern. Something is very, very wrong. I didn't want to worry you, but something strange and hard is growing in my breast."

She had not meant to blurt it out so bluntly, but the words had just tumbled from her mouth. Now she was too frightened to think clearly. It would be good to have Ernest's cool, professional hands touch her breast and tell her that there was no cause for alarm.

He stood there looking at her for a moment as if his shoes were glued to the floor. Finally the words came.

"Barbara, what are you saying?"

In a moment he was beside her, his fingers probing deep into her flesh. It only took him a minute, then he lay her head gently on the pillow. His face was white.

"The first thing tomorrow we must make an appointment for you at the hospital. I will call Dr. Haas tonight. . . . Oh, my dearest one, you should have told me a long time ago."

His arms went around her; his cheek was against hers, and Barbara felt the wetness of his tears on her cheek.

"Is it that bad, dear?" she asked, feeling strangely calm and distant.

He drew her closer.

"I don't really know yet; only the biopsy will tell. But we won't talk about it tonight, darling. I will call the doctor and make all the arrangements and give you a sleeping pill. The rest we'll leave in God's hands."

Barbara was too numb to speak. Ernest went downstairs and called Dr. Haas. Barbara heard his voice and felt the pain in it. She knew she must smile when he returned to her room. At least her problem would take his mind off Gail for a while. Then she heard him coming up the stairs.

"Here are two pills for you, dear. I want you to get a good night's rest."

"Will you take some, too, Ern? You must sleep, too."

He nodded and tucked the blanket in around her. She reached out her arms and he kissed her good-night.

"Everything is going to be all right," she told herself. "Ernest will see to that, and I must be brave for his sake."

Barbara fell into a deep sleep, and her anxious thoughts came to rest, along with her body. The night was bleak and cold and the stars seemed to add to the silence that had fallen over Golden Acre. Lady slept on her blanket beside the big double bed, but Ernest Omar, cancer specialist and surgeon, who had left his calling and retired in his prime, to find peace and happiness away from the tormented world of the city, sat on a chair in the bedroom with his head bowed. His hands were ice-cold and the sadness within him was more than he could bear.

How well he knew the symptoms! How many hundreds of women had he seen with the same signs, of whom he had asked the same question, "Why did you wait so long? Why didn't you come in the beginning, so I could have helped you?" But those were other women . . . not Barbara.

Barbara, he was thinking . . . it just couldn't happen to her. God must send down His Spirit to heal her. Dr. Haas's hands must be guided to remove any disease. Ernest's head bowed in prayer.

Oh, God, help us. I am just an unworthy human being, and I am unable to help the one I love most in the world. I know now that every woman I operated on has been just as precious to someone. You have given me the gift of healing through surgery. I left my calling to enjoy my years. Now, if only You will help, I promise to return to my practice, and whenever I operate, I shall remember this night and my plea to You for the one I love. Amen.

When morning began to dawn, he was still sitting there, numb with fear and sorrow. But Barbara's beautiful face was peaceful and composed in sleep. She seemed unaware of the danger that hung over her. How blessed was sleep.

Then Ernest Omar began to undress and soon quietly slipped into bed beside his wife.

10

Gail sat at the desk in her sunny room looking out at the high mountains which seemed to touch the blue sky. She loved those mountains, and she loved Earthend. This was just about the happiest place on God's earth, and she was lucky to live here. Presently, Gail's thoughts manifested themselves in words and she spoke them aloud.

"Grandma Olsen, are you there in the heavens somewhere looking after me? Have you talked to God about me? Is that why I ended up here instead of California? Is that why I met Douglas Rhodes and fell in love with him? Now my whole life has changed. It seems that I am becoming more of a convert to the truth each day. Doug doesn't just preach the Gospel . . . he lives it . . . and to be with him is to know the Word of God."

Gail had a strange feeling that her grandmother was close by and that God, in some mystical way, had sent down an angel to guide this granddaughter's every step. Everything was working out so beautifully. She and Doug had grown very close. He discussed important things with her and gave her a glimpse into his plans for

111

the church. And then sometimes just the way he looked at her was enough to send shivers up her spine. It was as if his eyes spoke to her instead of his lips, and they said so much. But most of all, they said what she wanted to know—that he loved her as she loved him. But since Doug was so openly honest, Gail was sure that he would not actually utter the words until she had confided in him and he knew the truth about her past.

Gail was now convinced that, before God, she had been wrong to worry her parents, to live under an assumed name, and to pretend that she was someone else. These convictions had come to her as she listened to Doug preach. He did not mince words, but spoke frankly, directly, and honestly. She had prayed to God to forgive her and promised that she would soon reveal her identity, but the days passed, and the mere thought that she might be separated from Doug kept her silent. She felt sure that as soon as he knew the truth, Doug would insist that she return to her parents. Perhaps he would not forgive her for the deception! Desperately she tried to think of the right words to use, but they would not come.

Gail's house-to-house visitations had been completed and there was no longer a need for them. The new preacher's popularity grew steadily and the word passed from one person to another of the strength he radiated from the pulpit. In fact, the church was so crowded on Sunday mornings that Doug had begun to hold two services. Earthend loved its Pastor Rhodes and he loved his flock. He surely was different from other ministers, Gail thought; he was different from anyone else in the whole world!

One particular day when Gail arrived at the church office, she had found Doug dressed in a pair of old slacks and well-mended jacket. He was on his way to chop firewood for Mr. Eldrich who was almost ninety and lived alone in a small house beside the highway. The three rooms of his cabin were heated by a single kitchen wood stove, and several cords of wood would be needed to get him through the winter. Until now, Mr. Eldrich had been taking care of his own wood supply, but Doug felt that the exertion was too great for the old man.

"I have dedicated part of this week to splitting wood for Mr. Eldrich," he told Gail. "That is, the part I can spare from my sick calls. I firmly believe that to serve my Master I must serve the people and that old man shouldn't put that much strain on his heart at his age."

Gail's admiration for her young preacher continued to grow. What a man he was! And what standards he had set for himself to follow—and what self-imposed disciplines. Was that why he limited his show of affection to simply holding her hand, she wondered. Was it against his principles to kiss a girl? Surely, ministers must have the same temptations as other men, and she wished that Doug would yield just a little.

Gail's next assignment had been to baby-sit for the children of a local mother who had to enter the hospital for a few days. Since there was no hospital in Earthend, Mrs. Samson had to travel to a nearby city where her husband worked in the coal mines. Gail had to be there at six o'clock in the morning and stayed until five in the afternoon.

She liked her baby-sitting job and she adored the children. There was a little girl of five with lovely curls, a happy little boy of three, and a baby who was not quite a year. They were affectionate and well-mannered children, and although the home was modest, it was immaculate and homey. Sometimes when Gail gave the baby his bottle, she would pretend that he was her baby and they lived in the parsonage with their daddy, who would soon be home, wanting his dinner. Those were happy hours, and occasionally Doug would drop in to say hello and play with the children. He never stayed for more than a few minutes, but his visits made Gail's day pass even more pleasantly.

"Gail, you are a girl of all trades," he had told her on one visit, in a voice that made her heart tremble. "Secretary—evangelist—now you seem to be the perfect little mother. See how the children love you. They probably don't even miss their own mother."

"That's because we have such fun together, and I tell them stories," said Gail. "But I'll bet that if their mommy were standing in the doorway, they would forget all about me."

Mrs. Samson was away only a week, then Gail moved on to another job.

"Your next assignment will be to go to stay with Mrs. Ball," said Doug. "She's a very old lady who is blind and who needs help feeding herself. Her daughter, with whom she lives, and who cares for her, needs some rest. So if you will go there, her daughter can take a few days' vacation. Mrs. Ball's sister will come in at five each afternoon and stay the night, so you can leave then."

"Okay. I guess I'll just change my uniform from that of baby-sitter to nurse. I'll bet there's no other minister's secretary who does the jobs I do!"

"I'm sure there isn't. Do you mind? Perhaps it isn't fair of me to expect you to do the things I feel should be done. If there's anything you don't want to do, just tell me."

Gail laughed happily. "Doug, the strangest thing is that I just love the diversity of my work. I'm learning so much and I have more fun meeting all these nice people. I assure you, I don't mind at all. The most fun is wondering what my next assignment will be."

The days passed—happy days for Gail, sometimes filled with hard work, but always rewarded by smiling faces, grateful hearts, and her own sense of accomplishment. Oh, it was good to be busy and to feel needed! Already she was part of the town, its people, and its activities. Gail's plans for college had dimmed in importance—for hadn't she found a calling in the world after all?

But there were some sharp regrets. Often, in the still of the evening, as she heard the infrequent passage of a car through town or a far-away train whistle, she thought of her parents and the pain they must still suffer from her disappearance. How she must have hurt them! Perhaps they even thought she was dead. In those quiet times Gail would vow to contact her family the next morning. Somehow, though, by dawn she would awaken to thoughts of Doug's probable reaction to the confession she would have to make to him of the lie she had been living, and she would allow herself to be swept into the new day's activities, her problem still unresolved.

The church continued to be crowded on Sunday mornings. Somehow the services sparked a revival of interest in other church activities—Bible study, Sunday school—even the youth were drawn by Doug's power.

"See how popular you are, Doug," beamed Gail. "I told you we would just move the whole town, but I never thought it would happen so soon."

"You deserve a great part of the credit, Gail," said Doug. "If you hadn't been so willing and capable, things never would have been done so quickly."

Gail was very pleased with Doug's praise.

The next Monday they spent together, going for a long ride to enjoy the beauty of autumn which had touched the wooded mountains, creating instant color everywhere. How Gail loved these rides. They were carefree and fun-filled and she felt an ever-growing bond between the two of them.

This particular Monday, Doug was in an especially good mood.

"How would you like to take off some Sunday afternoon in the next couple of weeks and drive with me to Vermont to see my grandmother?"

"I would love that," said Gail. "I hope she will like me."

"I'm sure she will and it's bound to be mutual. She is the dearest little lady, witty and filled with joy. And her old house is great! There are so many places I would want you to see."

"And I would walk in the woods with you, just like Jeff did."

"As soon as I can make the arrangements, we'll go. I'll write to my grandmother tonight."

They found a pleasant place to eat, and then it was time to start home again. Darkness came early, in October, and the trees were even now shedding their leaves, soon to stand in their nakedness waiting for the snow to arrive and clothe their bare branches. As they were driving along the almost deserted highway, they came upon a sheltered lake where a few ducks were lazily paddling. Doug pulled the car to the side of the road and stopped.

"I always carry a box of crackers with me in the car so I can feed the birds. How about giving those ducks a surprise evening snack?"

Gail was delighted and soon they were sitting on the grass at the edge of the lake, surrounded by hungry ducks.

They both laughed at the way the birds fought for and gobbled up every morsel. Soon the cracker box was empty, and the ducks departed. But Gail and Doug sat in stillness, watching the sunset which had turned the lake into a mysterious sea of gold. Everything in nature was quiet—a silent benediction on a perfect day.

"I don't know when I've seen a more glorious sunset," Gail half whispered. "But it will soon be dark. How quickly the darkness comes this time of year."

"Are you scared?"

"Not when I'm with you!"

"Good! You know I would protect you from whatever came along," said Doug, and playfully put his arm around Gail's shoulders. Gail leaned close to him.

This was the first time that Doug had, in any way, demonstrated his affection, and Gail could hardly believe it had happened. So she sat very still as if that would keep him from suddenly removing his arm.

For a while they sat silently looking into the fading sunset. It was as if the world stood still in peace and tranquillity. Gail had waited for this moment for so long. There was a oneness between them as if the two were alone in this magic world.

Then Doug spoke in a hushed voice.

"This has been such a perfect day, Gail. Why is it that when you and I are together, everything seems beautiful and right? I am very fond of you. I think I am in love, Gail."

"I think, perhaps, I am too."

He drew her close.

"Ever since the day I first saw you sitting there on that bench eating a sandwich, I think I have been in love with you. It seemed as if you dropped down from heaven, just for me."

"I was hoping you felt that way, because that's the reason I went with you to Earthend. I can't explain it, Doug. I don't know how something like this could have happened so quickly, but it did. I've loved you since that day, too."

"But, my dear, I don't even know if I have the right to love you. I've got to know your story—who you are, where you came from, and why you were sitting there alone—a girl from *Nowhere*. Please tell me now, Gail."

Gail didn't answer.

"Please, darling! Please."

But Gail just looked at Doug as if her eyes could explain the dilemma she was in. Then she felt them filling with tears.

The next moment Doug was kissing her tears away.

"Don't cry," he whispered.

Then his lips found her mouth, and tenderly his lips touched hers. It was a gentle kiss—more like comforting a child over a broken toy, than a lover's kiss. But to Gail it was the happiest moment of her life. She wanted to stay there in his arms, but a moment later he suddenly released her.

"Come on," he said. "We'd better go back to the car. It's getting dark."

Doug held her hand as they walked back and when they were in the car, she leaned her head on his shoulder. For a while they drove without speaking, as though they were slowly emerging from the spell in which they had been caught.

Doug spoke first. "I shouldn't have kissed you, Gail. I broke my own resolution, but I have wanted to for so long. My rule was that first you must trust me enough so that you would tell me all about yourself."

"I know," said Gail, "but I'm glad you let your iron will

slip for a few moments. I will tell you everything soon, Doug, I promise. But I need a little more time first. You see, it isn't just you to whom I must explain things, but now I have to decide what to clear up first."

He patted her shoulder lightly.

"I can wait, Gail. I know you will keep your word. But don't make me wait too long. You see, that parsonage is very large and I get very lonesome at times. But I'll trust your judgment."

It was only nine o'clock when they drove up in front of Mrs. Armstrong's house.

"Will you come in?" asked Gail.

"No, I think I'd better not. I have a lot to think about tonight and I have to write to Grandma, you know."

He gave her a light kiss, and she waved as he drove off.

Helen met her inside the door.

"I don't need to ask you if you had a good time, Gail. Your eyes are shining like stars."

"Does it show that much?" asked Gail.

"Did he propose?"

"No, not yet. But I'm sure he loves me. He's just a little cautious, but I can wait."

"Perhaps someone needs to give that bachelor-pastor a push. I think he has waited long enough."

"He is a man of principle—perhaps a little strange at times, but certainly worth waiting for."

Gail went up to her room early. She wanted to think and to relive the warmth of the last few hours. Now she no longer need wonder about Doug's love. It was up to her to make it blossom; and she *had* to decide what to do.

For a few minutes she considered using Helen's phone to call her parents—to tell them where she was and to warn her mother that she had better begin planning for a wedding! But soon Gail rejected the idea.

Her parents might be very angry. They might feel she was too young to think of marriage. They might even demand that she come right home. No, it would be better to wait and discuss it with Doug. The best thing would be to come clean—to start at the beginning—to tell him about her dream of Skidmore and how upset she had been when she had been denied her dream of college. She would tell him about Fran and Lynn and how they tried to help her—that she was not just running away aimlessly, but going to California to work herself through college. Now that she analyzed the whole thing, it didn't seem all that bad. She had just made herself out to be an awful ogre, but Doug would surely understand everything. She would tell him tomorrow. . . .

11

The plans that Gail had formulated so carefully did not materialize. When morning came, she was not able to tell Doug her story, and before the day was over, she had lost all desire to do so. It was all because of Linda Butler, whom Gail met for the first time that morning. Linda had been waiting outside the church when Gail arrived at exactly 9:00 A.M.

"I'd like to see Pastor Rhodes as soon as he comes in," she announced to Gail with a patronizing look. "By the way," she continued, "I am Linda Butler. You probably know my parents, the Stanley Butlers. We live on Sunrise Hill and they are members of this church."

"Of course," answered Gail with a friendly smile. "You must be the daughter who lives in New York City."

"That's right, but I have moved back home. The city is really becoming much too dangerous a place for a single girl to live. Last week a thief snatched my purse and scared me half to death, so I decided to leave my modeling job for a while and return to the old homestead."

"Welcome back! Pastor Rhodes should be here any minute. Would you care to wait in the office?"

The girls walked into the church office together, and Linda settled in a soft chair by the window.

"Sometimes the pastor runs an errand first, but I hope you won't have too long to wait. Make yourself comfortable."

A strange uneasiness filled Gail's heart. It was as if some instinct warned her that this chestnut-haired girl in her early twenties, with long dark eyelashes veiling emerald-green eyes, spelled trouble. There was something about her that annoyed Gail. It wasn't just that she was so lovely, and that her clothes were obviously too stylish and expensive to have been bought locally, but there was an air of cool self-confidence that was unsettling.

Everyone knew that Linda's banker-father was wealthy. Somewhere Gail had heard that Stanley Butler owned half the town, and she knew that the Butlers lived in a beautiful tree-shaded mansion with a swimming pool in their professionally landscaped yard—the only private pool in Earthend. Mrs. Butler was president of the Women's Club and socially active. The Butlers traveled often and entertained out-of-towners from as far away as the state capital.

However, their interest in the church had been slight—until Doug arrived. Gail had called on them during her visitations. She remembered approaching with curiosity the large brick house on Sunrise Hill. She had been met by a big, barking watchdog, but Gail managed to calm him down by speaking gently as she approached the front door and rang the bell. Mrs. Butler had opened it.

"Oh," she had smiled, "you are the new church secretary, aren't you? I had heard rumors that you were visiting all the homes in Earthend, but I never thought you would call on us. My husband already gives a substantial amount to the church. We don't always attend services because Mr. Butler likes to play golf on Sunday mornings and I am a late sleeper. But, believe me, we certainly stand one hundred percent in back of the new preacher."

"Well, this is by way of an invitation! Pastor Rhodes wants me to call on every home. It's important to him that we personally contact every church member first, and later all those who might like to become members."

They were still standing by the front door.

"Come in," invited Mrs. Butler. "It's nice of you to call."

Everywhere that Gail looked, luxury and elegance reigned. She sank down on a blue silk divan.

"I am here to invite you to come to our service on Sunday morning. This is the first time Pastor Rhodes is preaching in Earthend, and we want a full house. I think you'll like him and find his message worth hearing."

"Oh, we surely will be there! What a unique way to send out invitations—to send a pretty young girl in person."

"This is the way the pastor works, and I enjoy calling on people. Everyone has been so friendly and kind."

"It's nice to see a young girl in the service of the church. Our only daughter, Linda Ann, has been in New York a little over a year and a half now. She considers herself a career girl, and this town offers few opportunities for social life, as you may have noticed! Just now she is modeling for an old established agency. But we miss her."

"I hope she comes home occasionally."

"Not too often. She has an apartment and new friends in the city but Mr. Butler and I do go up to visit her sometimes."

They talked a little while longer, and the Butlers had been in church the next Sunday and every Sunday thereafter. And now Gail was meeting their daughter in person—the Miss Linda Butler. But what in the world did she have to see Doug about this early in the morning?

Soon Doug arrived and Gail introduced him to Linda. She seated herself assuredly opposite Doug's desk, and Gail kept busy on her own side of the room typing out some letters. Doug had smiled at Gail and her eyes had held his for a moment, reliving the magical night before, by the lake.

The conversation between Doug and Linda flowed smoothly. Gail listened with one ear to whatever was being said.

"I had to come this early," Linda was saying, "because I am playing golf with Dad at ten o'clock. But there is a favor I want to ask of you. There is a concert at Symphony Hall in Altoona tonight and we have tickets. Would you come as our guest? The whole family is going and we're having dinner at the Blue Mountain Inn before the concert. Please don't say no! I'd like to have the pleasure of getting to know you better as I plan to stay in town for a while."

"Of course. I'd be happy to accept. Thank you for thinking of me," Doug had answered all too readily, and, to Gail's annoyance, he had given Linda a wide smile.

They chatted for a while longer about time and place while Gail clicked away at her typewriter, not really knowing just what she was writing. She was fuming inside. On this special day, the first one after Doug had told her that he loved her, this beautiful creature had to come and spoil Gail's happiness. Linda was older, closer to Doug's age, and she was educated and rich. Gail had a strange feeling that she had a snare baited to catch the handsome new preacher. Gail had a rival, and she was very unhappy.

Finally, after Linda had swept out of the office, completely ignoring Gail as she passed, Doug came over to Gail's desk. He gave her a light kiss on the top of her head.

"And how is my girl today?" he asked.

"Just great," smiled Gail. She was certainly not going to let Doug know that jealousy was already raging inside her. "I hope you have a fine time with the Butlers tonight."

"I'm sure I will. How nice of them to extend me such a pleasant invitation, and delivered by such a beautiful young lady. I only wish they had included my secretary, too."

"I don't think that was on the Butlers' agenda. After all, I would be like a fifth wheel under the wagon. I'm sure Linda will help you forget my absence!"

"But I will miss being with you tonight, Gail. I hope you understand that there are many things that I, as a minister, must do, and I certainly don't want to offend the Butlers."

"I don't mind not being included," lied Gail, "but please don't let them take up any of our Mondays."

"I promise you that—Mondays belong just to the two of us."

Doug laid out the work for the day. He had quite a few visits to make, so soon Gail was alone in the office. As she typed up a speech for Doug, her mind wandered restlessly. She would not tell Doug about herself just yet, not now when Linda had come on the scene. Doug might feel that she had deceived him and that was something that Doug could not tolerate—lying and deceit. He had told her that himself one night when they had taken one of their long Monday drives and were headed toward home. They had been discussing young people and Doug had voiced his opinion clearly.

"There is one thing I cannot stand, Gail, and that is lying. To me, that is one of the worst sins in the world today. Perhaps I feel that way because of the way I was brought up, but to deceive a person by lying really irks me. People talk about white lies, but there is no such thing. Either something is true or it's not. I never again trust a person completely after I know that he has lied to me."

And that is the way Doug would classify her dishonesty—that her name was Gail Olsen. If only she had never said that. And the missing parts of her story—weren't they lies, too? It would have been better to use her real name no matter what happened. But how could she have known that then?

That night Gail talked about Linda with Helen Armstrong. Helen did not seem to hold too high an opinion of Linda Butler.

"She is spoiled rotten," Helen announced, "and as sure as I'm sitting here in this chair, I'll bet that her mother got her home to lay a trap for our preacher. Nothing would please Mrs. Butler more than to have her daughter become the wife of the minister in our now-so-prosperous church. I'll bet that she is already dreaming of building a new parsonage with all the luxuries that any house could offer. She wouldn't expect her daughter to live in our old parsonage! But we must not let that happen. Promise me, Gail, that you will hold on to him. He was yours first."

Gail laughed nervously.

"I surely don't want her to take Doug away from me, but I have so little to offer compared to the wealthy Miss Butler."

"Nonsense! What is money, after all. I don't think Douglas will fall for those fluttering false eyelashes. She is too much a girl of the world to suit him. But, of course, he can't snub the highest contributor to the church."

Helen and Gail played a game of checkers, but Gail's heart was not on the game. Her mind kept imagining Doug and Linda dining by candlelight in that romantic inn, probably feasting on pheasant or lobster, and then enjoying the concert together, sitting in the best seats, being encouraged by Linda's parents. After the concert he would certainly be invited to the Butlers' home for a late evening snack and there would be fun and laughter. Gail wondered if, in the midst of all that merriment, Doug would think of her, if he would remember holding her in his arms just the night before. It certainly was an unfortunate happenstance that Linda Butler had returned home just now.

That night Gail made up her mind that she would delay telling Doug about herself as long as she could. She wished that she were a little older. Perhaps she seemed like just a lost little girl to Doug now. Maybe his feelings were only those of a kindly benefactor toward a seemingly homeless stray. Hadn't he said she was a little like Jeff? She'd have to work at making him see her as a mature potential helpmate, lest he'd send her packing when he learned the truth.

But the next day Doug was completely himself. He laughed and joked and there was even time for a kiss or two. When she asked him about the concert, he said he had had a most enjoyable evening and that the Butlers certainly were a wonderful family, that Linda was a very talented girl, and that he had enjoyed her company. But he talked about the evening in such a detached manner that Gail's disposition improved immediately. Linda might be beautiful and talented and entertaining, but Gail had already captured Douglas Rhodes's heart, and since he was a special kind of man, she was sure that his love was true and she need have no fears. After all, she, too, came from a good prosperous family and as soon as she could tell Doug, she was sure he would be pleased with her background even though she lacked a college education. Still—the doubts remained—she'd better wait a bit longer.

After that evening, Linda Butler came often to the church office to see the pastor. She always seemed to have an errand at that end of town or a problem that only he could help her solve. And she had become suddenly zealous about church works. She had offered her soprano voice to the choir and asked if she could teach a Sunday-school class. Doug treated her with gentleness, courtesy, and encouragement, and readily returned her smiles. No matter how brave Gail was, her heart was heavy. Everything that had been so perfect had turned sour since Linda arrived.

Helen was even more disturbed than Gail.

"That girl has always had her own way," she told Gail. "As I said before, I'm sure that Mrs. Butler has put a bug in her ear about marrying the preacher. And I am telling you that Mrs. Butler will stop at nothing to get what her daughter wants."

"Don't worry, Helen," smiled Gail, with more courage than she felt. "I'm pretty sure of my preacher. Just give me a little more time, and I'll show Miss Butler that her scheme isn't working. Love will always find a way. You just wait and see."

But that night Gail changed her plans again. She had better have things out with Doug. As soon as her background was revealed, they could talk about marriage. So, on their next long ride—next Monday—she would tell Doug about herself, and after that, all the clouds would vanish from her sky. And Linda—well, she could just go back to the big city again.

12

Ernest Omar had a lengthy phone discussion about Barbara's condition with Herbert Haas. Dr. Haas was deeply concerned about Barbara and fully understood Ernest's justified fears.

"I will do my utmost for her, Ernest. You know that," he had said. "But it will be two more days before we can schedule her into the hospital. That's when the first private room will be available. You know how filled up the hospitals are these days."

"I know," answered Ernest. "Thanks, Herb, for doing your best. I'm almost beside myself with worry."

"Why don't you come down tomorrow and spend the night with us before Barbara checks in. Lois and Barbara will have a lot to talk about, and I think the change of scenery might do her good. It's best to keep her busy and occupied with more pleasant thoughts."

"I'll take you up on that, Herb. Thanks again. If for some reason Barbara objects, I'll call you back. Otherwise, we'll arrive tomorrow afternoon."

Barbara was comforted at the thought of spending a

night in their Lexington house. Her only concern was for Lady. They couldn't very well bring a dog along. Then Ernest suggested that they ask the Briggses to take her for a few days.

"Let's drive up the mountain this afternoon and explain our dilemma and ask if they will house Lady while we're away," he suggested.

Barbara thought that a fine idea.

"How long will I be hospitalized, Ern?" she asked, giving her husband an anxious look.

"That depends, dear," Ernest spoke tenderly. "If the biopsy is negative, you should be out in a couple of days. But if Herbert has to perform a mastectomy, you will have to stay for a couple of weeks to recuperate."

Barbara did not reply. Ernest's face revealed that he feared the worst. She tried not to panic. Why, many women had been in her predicament. Hundreds of them had lost a breast and still carried on, and she knew she was in good hands. But her thoughts went to Gail. She wondered how Gail would feel if she knew that her mother was going to the hospital. Would she try to contact them from wherever she was? If only there were some way Barbara could let her know.

Later in the day, they drove up the mountain road to the Briggses who were delighted to see them. Mrs. Briggs made coffee and they all sat in the kitchen to talk. Ernest told them about Barbara's impending hospital stay. They were sorry—very sorry—and Barbara could see that their eyes said what their lips did not speak. "It's that curse again," they seemed to say. "As long as you remain at Golden Acre, tragic things will continue to happen."

Barbara looked out over the valley. The trees were bare now, but there was a clean, structural beauty even in their bareness. She loved this spot where she could see for miles around the place she now called home. Why did so much sadness enter lives when the world was so full of beauty, sadness that sapped the joy and contentment from the soul? In spite of the unhappiness, everyone made an effort to be cheerful. Ernest asked about Lady, if she could stay with the Briggses for a few days, and they proved delighted to have her.

"Don't worry about a thing," said Mr. Briggs. "Mary and I will drive down to the Acre once a day and take a look around. Lady can go, too, and that will give her a feeling that she's not too far from home."

"We're very grateful," said Dr. Omar. "How lucky we are to have neighbors who are such good friends. I'll probably stay in Lexington for a few days so I can be near Barbara, and now I don't have to worry about either Lady or the house."

"Stay as long as you need to," said Mrs. Briggs.

Barbara took her hand.

"And, Mrs. Briggs, *if* Gail should come home and we are not there, I'm sure she will climb the hill to see her old friends. Tell her we'll be home soon."

"Nothing would please me more," sighed Mrs. Briggs. "How glad I would be if that happened."

Soon they were on their way down the mountain again, Golden Acre welcoming them from the midst of tall pines and leafless maples. The golden house surrounded by shrubs and a few remaining chrysanthemums was an impressive sight as they rounded the bend. It had come to mean a great deal to the Omars.

"Now I want you to put on your prettiest outfit, Mrs. Omar," laughed her husband. "I'm going to take you out for dinner tonight, and we shall go to a romantic place. How about High Point Inn? It's just far enough for a nice ride, and they have excellent food and candlelight."

Barbara dressed in one of Ernest's favorites, a new red-and-white pantsuit which showed off her trim figure. She was careful as she put on her makeup. She wanted to look her very best, as this night would mean a lot to them both. Was it to be another new beginning—or was there more sorrow ahead?

They dined in style on broiled lobster and tasty side dishes, topping off their meal with a very rich pecan pie and whipped cream, drizzled with native maple syrup. For a while the flickering candle flames soothed their troubled spirits and it was possible to push back the fears of tomorrow, and even the ache of their daughter's disappearance.

But the next day arrived quickly, and soon they were on their way to Lexington, with an extra bag packed for Barbara's stay in the hospital. She tried not to think about what was in store for her, but the alarming thoughts came now and then. She knew she would be relieved when the ordeal was over—whatever the verdict.

It was strange, returning to their former home, to see how well Lois Haas had taken care of it. Since it was a crisp fall night, there was a fire blazing in the living room. Barbara felt as though the house silently reached out its arms to welcome them home. Lois had prepared an excellent dinner.

"It feels good to be home," Ernest said, as they sat down in the dining room.

"Yes, I know how you must feel," smiled Lois. "This has been a good home for us, too. It is a lovely house."

"But we have some news to tell you," her husband added. "We have fallen in love with a new house, quite a bit smaller, and I have a bid on it. You see, with help so hard to get, this place is a little too big for Lois to handle. I didn't mean to bring this up right now, but I know that you will want to make plans, if we move out."

"That isn't such bad news," said Barbara. "We might just move back here for the winter. I don't like the idea of being snowed in up there in the wilderness, no matter how much I love our Golden Acre. Winter is another thing."

"Yes," said Ernest Omar, "we might just move back if you find another place. And another thing, Herbert. I think your senior partner will soon be back in the office. I have decided to go back to work again. The rest was good for me, and I do love the White Mountains, but I have to confess that when this happened to Barbara, I realized how much the world needs dedicated doctors. It's selfish of me not to use my operating skills when I still have my health. We will always keep Golden Acre as a second home, and it will be a great retreat for the summer months. But if you *do* move out, we will move in."

Herbert laughed. "That was a short retirement, Doctor Omar! But I need a partner. The office hours keep getting longer each day. I welcome the news of the senior partner's return."

"It's strange. Sometimes something unpleasant has to hit you before you wake up to the fact that you are needed in this world."

The four friends spent an enjoyable evening together, and when they retired for the night, Barbara had no fear for the next day.

The Haases had given Ernest and Barbara their old bedroom for this visit, and it seemed as if time had rolled back and that the months in New Hampshire had never been.

Again Ernest insisted that Barbara take a sleeping pill,

even though she was sure there was no need. But she took the pill to please him and soon she was sound asleep.

Ernest sat in a chaise trying to read, but soon he let the magazine drop to his lap as he gazed at Barbara sleeping as peaceful as a child in the big double bed. He was satisfied that he had been able to hide the fears he felt, but now they returned with renewed force. What if the lump was malignant, he thought, and suddenly he felt totally powerless to help the one he loved most in the world.

Ernest Omar stared at his hands as if he had not really seen them for a long time. They were rough from chopping wood and baiting fishhooks and working in the garden, but the long tapered fingers still spoke of the skill they knew when they held a scalpel, ready to cut into the flesh of a sick person there on the operating table. The blood in his veins tingled at the thought of operating. What a challenge to detect the diseased part of the body, to remove it, and to witness the healing powers —restoring health, hope, and happiness. Surely this was what God wanted him to do!

Ernest began to think back in his memory file of all the grateful ones who had returned to pour out their thanks with glowing eyes.

"Doctor Omar," one might have said, "thank you for making me well. Words can never express how deeply grateful I am."

He had taken their outstretched hands and felt unworthy of their praise even though their words warmed his heart.

"I'm glad for you," he might have answered, "but I only did what I've been trained to do."

But then there were those who had not pulled through. How could he erase from his memory the first case he had lost? He had been young then, and so confident and sure of his abilities. The operation had not seemed serious, but an infection had set in and had sped with lightning speed through her body. The patient had been a young woman who always greeted him with a warm smile. She had trusted him completely. Ernest had been heartbroken and defeated when the woman died suddenly, leaving a fine husband and two small children. Where had he failed? He had asked himself that question over and over. It had preyed on his nerves and he had gone to see the Chief of Surgery at the hospital.

"Where did I fail?" he had asked.

Dr. Spoon had patted his shoulder. "Don't blame yourself. I'm sure you did all you could. It just happened. We doctors are not God. Our powers are limited. There are times when no human efforts can save a life, but we still have to stand tall and know that we tried our best. We have to tell ourselves that we did everything we could. Then we continue to research new cures and try new methods; our desire for additional knowledge never ends. The science of medicine never takes a holiday. One day we hope we will have found the remedy for all disease."

"But she was too young to die. She had children who need her, and she trusted me. It seems so useless to think I tried my best and failed."

"You have learned a valuable lesson today, but now you must learn to master your emotions. As the years pass and you become a veteran surgeon, you will have learned that you cannot grieve over every loss. If you learn this from the beginning, you will be a better doctor. To master yourself is an important factor."

Ernest Omar had always been grateful for Dr. Spoon's

advice. Through the years he had learned to insulate himself against failure and to stand tall when the inevitable happened. He accepted the fact that in his profession there would always be a struggle between victory and defeat, between life and death. All he could do was his best.

But that attitude was easier when it happened to other people with names like Adams, Baxter, or Dixon—names that paraded alphabetically in his files. This was different because it was Barbara. For the first time it occurred to him that every person he had operated on had been a *Barbara* to someone. Others had lived through the agony that now tortured his mind. They must have prayed and waited and trusted that God would stand by that operating table.

Ernest knew just one thing tonight—he could not live without her; she was his whole life. Barbara and Gail. Gail had left them. How they needed her now. Where was she? Was she dead or alive? Would he ever know? He had prayed so fervently for her return, but his prayers did not seem to be answered. Was it because he had been neglectful about prayer, before, although he at times breathed one during a difficult surgery? Or was it God's will that they loosen the protective cocoon in which they had wrapped their daughter? Would that they had not been so selfish—it was their own desires, not Gail's, which he and Barbara had sought to fulfill.

Now he felt so helpless. What a wonderful married life he and Barbara had spent together, he was thinking. They had had a short courtship, for the moment he first saw Barbara he had desired her for his wife.

She had been vacationing in Boston with a group of graduate students from her college in Minnesota, when Ernest met her at a concert. Barbara had twisted her ankle

on a slippery floor during the intermission and the man-
agement had called for a doctor. He had come forward
and they had ushered him into a small lounge where
Barbara was sitting on a couch. She had smiled up at him
with those wide blue eyes, the clearest he had ever seen.
Her complexion had been a flawless soft pink and her hair
a delicate ash blond, so typical of the Scandinavian people. He had wanted to touch her cheek just to feel the
softness of it. Her voice was low and melodious as she
apologized for disturbing him.

"This is so silly," she had said. "They shouldn't have
called you away from the concert. Now you will miss part
of it. I just stepped on something wet and slipped. I'm
sure my ankle isn't that bad, but our guide wanted to be
sure there are no broken bones, since we're traveling
back to Minneapolis tomorrow."

He had examined her foot carefully and found nothing
broken, but had hurried to his car to get his bag and then
tenderly bandaged her slender ankle. He found himself
wondering how he could get in touch with her again, and
then he had an idea. He could get her address so he could
find out how her ankle had mended. He had been relieved when he found that her name had been *Miss* and
not *Mrs.* Their courtship had begun with letters and then
one day he had flown out to Minnesota to meet her parents, the dearest people anywhere, living in a charming
old house filled with wood carvings and copper kettles
from the old country. Ernest had liked Mr. and Mrs. Olsen
from the start, and they seemed fond of him, too. After that
he spent many weekends in Minnesota and each time he
saw Barbara, he loved her more. Ernest had dated many
girls, but with Barbara Olsen he had known from the
beginning that she was *The One*.

After she graduated, they had married and moved into

an apartment in Boston for a while and then, as his practice grew, they had bought the house in Lexington and
furnished it little by little until it was just the way they
planned. Even now they maintained the newness of their
relationship. Ernest still felt a thrill at Barbara's touch and
the sense of admiration which he had felt for her that first
meeting.

How did the Scriptures picture the virtuous woman?
Barbara was all that and more: patient, wise, kindly, di-
ligent, yes—but as the wife of a pressure-ridden and
sometimes testy doctor, she had so beautifully revealed
all those qualities "more precious than rubies" which had
made their years together so fulfilling. It was a wonder
how she managed to complement his own busy existence,
and yet maintain her own identity. Alert and alive to the
world and people around her, she had been the most
wonderful wife any man could have.

They had waited five years for Gail. They had been
impatient that a baby had not come sooner, but when she
finally arrived, their joy knew no bounds. Gail was as
beautiful as her mother, with the same blue eyes. And she
had been happy and obedient and dear in every way.
Then they had spoiled it by not letting her enter college.
Although this had been done out of love, Gail had not
understood their motives. Then Ernest had retired from
surgery, leaving behind his vocation, and he had found
his Golden Acre. Never in his wildest imagination did he
dream that Gail would take the situation into her own
hands and leave them without giving them the opportun-
ity to change their minds. And when they *had* changed
them, it had been too late. The summer had been wonderful, but it would have been more nearly perfect if they had
let Gail choose her own way of life. But he could

not undo what had been done. And now there was Barbara . . . . He glanced at her again—her face so beautiful and calm. Ernest wanted to embrace her, to cover her face with kisses, but he dared not. She needed her rest for the morning when Herbert would operate. Then they would know the full story.

As he sat there thinking, Ernest felt the need to pray.

O God, let me keep her. Please, Lord, be merciful to me, and I promise that I will dedicate my life to helping others, that each person I operate on will be as important to me as Barbara. I promise this with my whole heart. Give me back the two I love—my wife and my daughter. Wherever Gail is, protect her from harm and shield her from evil. O God, I wish I had words to express what I feel in my soul. Sorrow has taken over. I wish I could say "Thy will be done," but I want *my* will done. I have to be honest. So I plead for the dearest and most sacred part of my life to be healed. Hear me, mighty Creator. Amen.

A calm came over Ernest and he realized that he, too, had to prepare himself for the day to come and in a few moments he was resting beside Barbara in the old Lexington bed.

Among the White Mountains, in New Hampshire, Golden Acre stood deserted. A half-moon threw an eerie glow over the yellow house. And on top of the mountain, Lady slept in the corner of the kitchen in the Briggs's old house, wondering, perhaps, what had happened to her master and mistress.

The world was silent, concealing the future that would soon unfold. It was as it had been since the world was first created—the story of man and his struggle with sickness and health, with wrong and right. The world which God had created as a beautiful paradise had gone off course, but at some time, through sorrow and trial, man would find his way again, back on the only road that leads to joy and peace.

13

Early one morning Helen Armstrong knocked on Gail's bedroom door, announcing that there was a telephone call for her. Gail looked at the clock and wondered who would be calling her at seven o'clock. But Helen quickly answered her thoughts.

"He's on the phone, Gail—your pastor."

There had been a big grin on Helen's face as though her news were the happiest message she could bring her friend. But Gail was alarmed. Why in the world would Doug call her so early? She almost flew to the nearest phone in Helen's bedroom.

"Doug?" she asked, with pounding heart.

"Good morning, Gail!" came his deep voice, so dear to her ears. "I'm sorry to awaken you this early, but I had some bad news during the night. My dear little grandmother has had a stroke, and I'm leaving for Vermont right now."

"Oh, I'm so sorry, Doug. Let's pray that she will come through it."

"We'll leave that in God's hands. But you will have to

take over, dear. Stay in the church office in the morning. I've left some letters for you to type for me. Then in the afternoon would you go to the parsonage and tidy up a little? That is, if you don't mind. When I return, I'll look forward to your homey touches, and I'm sure you can do it."

"Of course I can, Doug, and I'll love every moment of it. Please call me at the parsonage this afternoon so I'll know how your grandmother is."

"I promise, and I'll be back as soon as I can. I know you'll look after things."

"Have a safe trip, Doug, and bring back good news!"

After Gail had shared the message with Helen, she went back to her room and sat down on the edge of the bed. Oh, how she prayed that Grandmother Rhodes would be well again. Gail wanted so much to meet her. It would be almost like having her own grandmother back again. If only she could have gone with Doug, to sit beside him those many miles. But now she would not be able to tell him her predicament; she would have to wait a few more days before she would feel completely free to call her mom and dad. It would be good to hear their voices, to feel that there was nothing to hide, and to assume her own name. She wondered how Doug would handle things. How would they explain to Helen Armstrong and the church members? But she knew that she wouldn't have to worry about it. Doug would find a way; she could leave it to him.

Gail crept under the covers and for a while she just lay there, trying to sort out her own thoughts. Just a little over two months had passed since she had left home, but she felt as if she had lived a whole lifetime. She could not imagine how life had been without Doug, and now that she knew he loved her, her heart was so filled with happiness that she could wish for no more. To go to college was no longer important. In fact, she would just drop the idea if Doug wanted to marry her immediately. She would suggest that she might complete her education gradually; she could take courses wherever they were available in this part of the country. She was sure her father would give her a car for a wedding present if she suggested it. Then she could commute to the nearest school. She had a feeling that Doug would want his wife to have a good education, but she hoped he didn't make her wait until hers was completed before he married her.

Oh, how much she wanted to be Mrs. Douglas Rhodes and to move into that parsonage. She would try to be such a good minister's wife, so he would be proud of her. Of course, Mom and Dad might object to her being married at eighteen, but she was sure she could talk them into understanding. They would be so glad to have her back—and how could they do anything but love Doug? They couldn't wish for a more wonderful man for her to marry.

Gail left her bed and began to dress and soon she was sitting at the table having breakfast in Helen's cozy kitchen. Helen was all smiles.

"I've never seen you look happier, Gail. Are you hiding something from me?"

"You know I wouldn't hide anything from you, Helen," answered Gail lightly. "I promise that when I have good news, you will be the first to know. Doug just asked me to tidy up the parsonage for him while he was gone. So after a little office work this morning, that's where I will be."

"Do you want me to help you?"

"No, not at all. Thanks just the same. It will be fun to practice a little housework. May I pick a few mums from your garden and borrow a vase? I'd like to put some flowers on the coffee table in the parsonage living room. I think Doug would like that."

"Just help yourself. Pick all you want. Anything I can do, just let me know. I'll bake an apple pie, and you can stick that in his refrigerator. I hope his grandmother isn't too bad and that he'll be back soon. Earthend will seem strange now without our wonderful pastor."

And the office seemed strange too. It was very lonely without Doug. How terribly Gail missed him already. The letters didn't take long to type, and then Gail dusted and picked up the office. There were a few sick calls, but Gail explained about Doug being gone to each person who called and recorded their names. When Gail came home to lunch, Helen had the pie ready. Gail picked the flowers, an arm-filling bouquet, and found a muted green vase. Then Helen drove her to the parsonage which was a short distance away. Doug had left the key in the mailbox and Gail waved good-bye to her friend and let herself in the front door. She stopped in the hall to read a note on the table.

Dear One,
    I wish you could have gone with me today. I shall miss you. I'll call you later today when I've seen my grandmother.

All my love,
DOUG

Gail hugged the note to her heart. He felt the same way she did about being apart, and best of all, he would call her this afternoon. She could hardly bear so much happiness, but now she must busy herself straightening up his home. What fun that would be! Gail arranged the flowers and placed them on the coffee table. They really brought a difference to the whole room; the vase was just right, too.

It didn't take very long to finish. Gail discovered that Doug was very orderly and everything was in place. But she dusted the furniture and ran the vacuum cleaner over the rugs. There were no dirty dishes in the sink, so Gail just shined things up a little, wondering how it would feel to be Mrs. Rhodes, taking full-time care of the parsonage. It was far too large for just the two of them, she was thinking, but it was a sunny, pleasant house, painted yellow on the outside just like Golden Acre. The furniture was comfortable though not luxurious, but it would do. She would change the curtains, she thought, and get something that fitted all those windows, and she would add drapes in the living room, and perhaps a braided rug, if Doug could afford it. There was a large raised hearth in the living room and she was sure that this would be their favorite place to sit watching the flames on long winter nights. The master bedroom had just a single bed—that would have to be changed, too, she thought. There were other bedrooms on the second floor, but only Doug's was furnished. The rooms on the second floor were vacant at present, and the doors were closed so they didn't have to be heated. The pastor who had preceded Doug had eight children and had used every inch of space. Helen had told her the parsonage had showed a great deal of wear-and-tear during the time that this large family used it. After they had gone, the whole parsonage had been renovated and the walls were given new paper and paint, inside and out. Most of the furniture had been discarded, but now the parsonage was clean and the sun shone brightly through the large windows.

"I'm sure I could make this house such a pleasant home," Gail said to herself. "I know just what I would need to make it perfect for Doug and me."

When she was through with her work, Gail sat down on the living-room sofa to wait for Doug's call. There was lots of reading material, but Gail didn't feel like reading. She wanted to recount what had happened during the short time that she and Doug had known each other.

Gail recalled some conversations they had had on their Monday drives. Once they discussed doctors, and she had almost given herself away as she had tried to defend the modern doctor. It had all started out with Gail's remark to Doug when he had been talking about his grandfather.

"I think you would have made a fine doctor, Doug," she had told him. "Someday you might be sorry that you didn't follow in your gramp's footsteps."

"No, I'll never be sorry," he had assured her. "After living with Gramp and watching him work, giving of himself to his people, I could never be a modern doctor, collecting astronomical fees and giving people so little for their money."

"Not all doctors are like that," Gail had protested. "I know men who have devoted their lives to people, but in a different way. Did you ever stop to think of what it costs to start out in medicine today—all that equipment, an office, and nurses— things that your gramp never had to have. I'll bet he just had his black bag and that his office was just a room in his house, with no nurse."

Doug had stared at her for a moment.

"That's true," he said slowly. "Gramp may just have had his trusty old black bag and no fancy office, but he had a heart. He felt for people, and when patients didn't have the money for his bill, he conveniently forgot it. His aim was to serve humanity, not to make money. Time meant nothing to him—he never counted the hours."

"Don't you think today's doctors have any heart for people? They don't *have* to give their service, but many do more than necessary. They don't *have* to worry about their patients or walk the floor at night, wondering how to save a life, but some do. Their hours are long, too. Emergency operations occur and they have to leave their families no matter what has been planned, just to answer their calls. Sometimes the strain is so great that they have to go away to rest in order to return fresh and alert."

"You certainly seem to know a great deal about doctors! I suppose you're right. I might have misjudged the medical profession of today after having lived with Gramp. You see, to me, he outranked all other doctors."

Gail felt the blood rush to her face. In her outburst, she had forgotten to guard her speech. Perhaps she had said too much, but for the moment, the excellent service and long hours her own father had put in had made it mandatory that she defend him.

"I did have a very wonderful doctor who cared for me," she said softly, "and I wanted you to know that there are men in medicine who give their lives to humanity, even though they make more profit than an old-fashioned country doctor." She smiled at Doug. "I still think you would have made an excellent doctor, even in these modern times."

"But I love being a minister, and I really feel that I can help more people by speaking the Word and helping to save their souls, which are often more sick than their bodies, you know. Sometimes I wish that I could heal their hearts, but only God does that. All I have to do is to lead the soul-sick to Him."

"Your ministry is so different from any other I've ever experienced. Do you think you could operate the same way if you had a large metropolitan church?" asked Gail, relieved that they had changed the subject.

Doug was quiet for a while as if he were pondering a problem that had plagued him many times before.

"I don't know, Gail, how much I would be permitted to

do in a large parish. You see, that is one reason I wanted my first church to be in a small town, far from city life. I wanted to try my own way of serving God. I think I'm doing the right thing. I'm not working for the money. I hope I'm giving something of myself and my talent to my people and that I'm giving them some understanding of God's way for the world. People need to be taught to think, in the busy days in which we live. Most people don't really think; they just follow the crowd. If one demonstrates, half the followers don't really know what they are agitating for or against—they just follow. This is a mad world, and we can't let this insanity take over. Christ says we should "overcome evil with good," and that's what I'm trying to do. And it works, Gail; it really works! Already I have seen the fruits of my labor. If I had a larger church, a more sophisticated one, I couldn't help by chopping wood. But here, I can always find a feeble person who needs a ride or I can lend a hand in other humble ways. That is my task as a minister of God."

"Yes," Gail had said, "I think you are doing the right thing. I admire the way you serve your people and the town is certainly a better place because you are here."

Their Monday rides had been filled with important learning for Gail. If she was going to be a minister's wife, she would want to work along with Doug. It would probably mean giving up the relative luxury to which she was accustomed. She was sure it would mean toil and sacrifice, but how willing she was to accept all of this. Just now it seemed to be the only way to live. Gail was amazed at how much she had changed in such a short time. The key to life, she thought, is to give of yourself to others— to laugh, to love, and to lift, producing such happiness that nothing could equal it. How glad she was that she had met Doug and come here with him.

Gail glanced at the tall clock in the living room. It was almost five o'clock. Doug should be calling any minute now. He must have reached Vermont some time ago, and probably he had found time to reach the hospital.

But still another hour passed before the telephone rang. Doug's voice crackled on the other end.

"I was trying the parsonage first," he said. "If there had been no answer, I would have called Helen's house. How are things in Earthend?"

"Everything here is fine. The parsonage is spic-and-span, though there wasn't much to do. You are a very neat man, Pastor Rhodes."

"Thanks for the compliment. It's good to have you there, Gail. Grandmother had a slight stroke, and although her voice is a little thick and garbled, most of the time I can make out what she's saying. The doctor says there is very little brain damage, and he feels she will come out of it before long. But she should not be living alone so far away from me. So, as soon as she is able to travel, I will bring her to Earthend."

"Oh, that will be wonderful, Doug. We will have a grandmother here, and I can share her with you. I'm so glad she'll be all right. When are you coming home?"

"I'll start back in the morning. I can't wait to see my girl."

"And I can't wait to see you! It has been lonely here without you."

"That sounds good. Take care of things till I get home."

They said good-bye and Gail hung up the receiver. She felt warm and contented. Now she would meet Grandmother Rhodes, and when she and Doug were married, Doug's grandmother could spend her last years with them. Everything was working out perfectly, and as soon as Doug knew who she really was, life could begin to take shape again. Gail knew that she had found her place on earth. This was *her* Golden Acre, she thought. Everyone must be looking for his own special place, and she had to travel pretty far to find hers. But she aimed to make it a good life with Doug there to guide her.

As Gail walked back to Helen's house from the parsonage, darkness was beginning to fall over the town. In the distance stood the mountain peaks, now dark and oppressive. But there was no danger here. True, the town had its small share of minor delinquency and crime, but the incidents were few, and people walked back and forth to their homes unafraid, even at night. Gail walked past the church and stopped for a moment. The white steeple, with its cross, pointed to the heavens, and a beacon blinked through the night to remind people of the love of God. How much she loved this town and its people—how much a part of her they had all become.

Gail remembered the first time she had seen the church and how it had brought solace to her troubled heart. Now, after all these weeks, the church was even dearer still. A church should be the very center of a town, she mused. Never before had she realized how important was God's House to a community.

This church had become a refuge to its people, especially now that it had come alive under Doug's guidance. It seethed with activity and on Sundays every pew was filled with people eager to hear Doug preach. His every word spoke of the love of God and was delivered from the depths of his honest soul.

Winning people for God was Doug's aim, instilling in them the peace that surpassed all human understanding. All this flowed from the pulpit, where Doug stood tall and handsome in his black robe every Sunday morning. Her heart filled with joy at the thought.

As she neared Helen's house, she saw bright lights and knew that her friend was waiting with a good dinner for her. They would talk and laugh and watch television together and then Gail would go up to bed. Then, on the new day, Doug's car would come driving up the street and she would be there at the parsonage to meet him. And when she was in his arms again, everything would be right with the world. The nagging weight of her secret would be lifted, as she cleared up the mystery of her past for the man she loved. And best of all, she'd talk to Mom and Dad again!

14

And what are your plans for today, Gail?" asked Helen, as the two of them finished their breakfast.

"Well, first I have to go to the church office and be a secretary for a while, answering the telephone and taking down messages for Doug. And in the afternoon, because my boss has given me no specific assignment, I shall go and make a few sick calls. I know that when Pastor Rhodes returns to his flock, he will want to know how its bedridden members are faring. So I'll check on them."

Helen began to clear the kitchen table.

"And what time do you think your Pastor Rhodes will be back in Earthend?"

"Not until dinner time. He has hundreds of miles to cover and it will take hours, even if the roads are good."

"How about inviting him here for dinner tonight?"

Gail put her arms around her friend.

"Oh, Helen, you are a dear. I know Doug would like that. After spending his time between that lonely house in Vermont and visiting his grandmother in the hospital, he will appreciate being in a warm home. I'll leave a note for him in the office. Very likely he'll stop in there first."

As Helen washed up the dishes after Gail had left, she could not help but think how lucky she was to have found a young friend like Gail Olsen. Now there was always some activity in her old house, and the preacher visited Helen's house more often than any other house in the town. Helen had a hunch that before too long Gail would be leaving her and moving over to the parsonage! Helen was sure that from the way that young lady's eyes were shining lately, Gail was very likely dreaming of wedding bells.

It wasn't very long before Helen had a pumpkin pie in the oven. Douglas Rhodes was very fond of her pies and this was just the right day for baking. The air was crisp and clear, and by nighttime there might be a heavy frost. This was that time of year which Helen loved most. It felt good to have a sturdy, warm house with friendly people coming and going. Most people in Earthend were friendly by nature, especially the mailman. John Hall was everyone's friend, Helen observed, as she saw him coming up the path to the back door. He must have a package for her. Otherwise, he just left the mail in the box by the road. But if there was a package, he made himself very important and came to the door with it, hoping to be invited in. Once inside he would sit down for a chat. Today John had a large carton in his arms.

"It's from California," he announced, as he set it down on the kitchen table.

"Oh, thank you, John. It's from my brother Carl. He moved out there when he retired. He has taken up wood-carving and promised me a fancy breadboard."

When Helen didn't volunteer to open the package, the mailman left reluctantly. Helen had purposely waited until he left; she was not going to encourage him to stay. It might start a bad habit! But he had left with a cheery good-bye.

When she was alone, she quickly tore off the paper, and there it was—wrapped in layers of newspaper—the most beautifully carved breadboard she had ever seen. It was really too nice to hide. She'd have to find a place for it on her kitchen wall. Carl certainly had a talent for carving.

After she had admired her gift, she straightened out the newspapers. She glanced through them casually. It was always fun to see what was happening in other parts of the country. She sat down on a kitchen chair and spread the papers out on the table and began to thumb through them. Suddenly the blood rushed from Helen's face. She stared at a picture on the third page of the paper. She could not believe it, but it must be . . . . There was a picture of Gail. If it wasn't Gail, it surely must be her twin.

There was an article under the picture and Helen pondered the black type:

BOSTON DOCTOR SEARCHES FOR DAUGHTER

On the fifteenth of August, in the early morning hours, Gail Omar left her parents' summer home in New Hampshire, leaving a note indicating that she was starting out to make her own way in life. There had been a family misunderstanding, causing a rift in their relationship. No trace has been found of her in spite of an extensive search by the police and private detectives. If anyone has knowledge of the whereabouts of Miss Omar, please contact her family or local police.

This was followed by an address.

Helen sat glued to her chair. That was Gail all right! The date of her disappearance was the same date she had arrived in Earthend. Douglas must have picked her up somewhere along the way, unless he was in on it. What was the world coming to anyway? Could there be a reason in back of her running away? Could their pastor know this girl? Was he helping her run away from home? Helen was hot and cold all over, and for the life of her, she could not think of what she should do.

She took her pie out of the oven, and then she picked up the newspaper and read the article once again, looking intently at the picture of the lovely young girl whom she thought she knew so well and whom she had learned to love as a member of her own family. What to do now was the question. Should she call Mr. Morrison, the church moderator? Should she speak to Gail, or just wait until Pastor Rhodes returned and then leave it all in his hands? Finally, Helen decided on the latter.

The grandfather's clock in the living room chimed ten times. Suddenly Helen remembered that she was to attend a board meeting of the Ladies' Guild, and here she was, still sitting at home. Well, it certainly had been an exciting morning. Just now she didn't feel much like going, but she had a report to give, so she had better be there. She glanced once again at the newspaper spread out on the kitchen table. Since she would be gone only a little over an hour, she would leave it where it was until she returned. Then she would cut out the article and give it to Douglas. But right now, she had to hurry.

As Helen drove the short distance to the meeting, she decided not to say a word about her discovery to any of the ladies. It would have to be her secret until she had talked to her pastor and gotten his advice.

It was under two hours when Helen returned, and now she carefully cut the article out of the paper and disposed of the scraps. Then she began to fix lunch for Gail and herself. It would be strange eating with her friend, knowing that she was not an Olsen but an Omar. But Helen decided to try to look gay and act like her old self. Somehow she couldn't face the embarrassment of revealing what she knew to Gail.

But the noon hour passed and Gail did not appear. Well, that had happened before, especially when Helen had been away and not been able to answer the phone. Helen ate her lunch alone, but her mind was hardly on what she was eating. She was not used to facing such problems, and this one seemed like a big dark cloud descending on her happy household. She prayed it would not spoil their happiness. Now Helen waited for Douglas to return; with his wisdom and tact he would surely know what to do.

Fortunately she did not have to wait very long before she saw the small sports car pull into her driveway. She was at the door waiting for him before he had time to ring the bell. He looked well and was smiling.

"Hi," he said. "I came here because my secretary is nowhere to be found. There was a note on my desk though, saying you had graciously invited me for dinner tonight. Thank you. I accept with pleasure. I'm back a little early because I left Vermont in the wee hours of the morning. I was very anxious to get back to Earthend."

"And you are so welcome back. Gail is evidently making some sick calls for you. She didn't come home for lunch, so I'm sure that means she is quitting early."

"Bless her," said Douglas. "My grandmother is so much better, thank God for that. She is a dear old soul and I love her very much."

"My goodness," said Helen, "here we are, still standing by the door. Come into the living room. Start a fire in the fireplace if you'd like one."

"I'd love to do just that," beamed Douglas. "It is good to be back."

While he laid the fire, Helen collected her thoughts.

With the fire blazing, Doug sank down onto the sofa, and a minute later, Helen was sitting beside him.

The living room was hushed. Doug gave Helen a puzzled look.

"Ever since I arrived here this afternoon, I have had the strangest feeling that something is wrong," he said.

"You are right, and this is what it is," said Helen as she handed him the newspaper clipping. She watched his face as he read it, wishing in her heart that this were just a dream.

Douglas put the clipping down on the side table. His face was pale.

"So that was her story," he said as though he was talking to himself. "You see, I picked her up that day I drove to Earthend. It isn't my policy to pick up hitchhiking girls, but I met her at a rest area on the road. She seemed too nice to be thumbing a ride, so I took her along. You know Gail's winning ways. And when she expressed a desire to work without pay, I thought this would be a good place for her—to give her time to find herself. I might get into trouble now for not finding out more about her, but she refused to tell me anything about herself."

"She should be here any moment," said Helen. "Perhaps she will be able to explain a lot of things to us now. She has been a wonderful helper to you and a good friend to me, don't let us forget that."

"I'm afraid I am in love with her."

"To me that is good news, an answer to my prayers. I have been dreaming of seeing the two of you together in our parsonage."

"I think I'll go home for a while and rest, Helen. I'll be back at six."

"That's a good idea, Pastor Douglas. I'll take a little rest myself before Gail comes back."

After Helen had walked Doug to the door, she climbed the stairs to her room, and it was then that she found the note Gail had pinned to her bedspread.

Dear Helen,

I came home unexpectedly about 10:30 A.M. and I saw the article in the paper. I am crushed and ashamed. I have caused you much trouble and embarrassment. I am leaving Earthend. Thank you so much for everything and give my love to Doug. Please forgive me.

GAIL OMAR

That was all. Helen turned the paper over. Where could the girl go? It was fall and growing cold now, not like summer when she had left home. But everything had been too perfect. Life had been like a song, but it just didn't stay that way. Even with Linda Butler's arrival from New York, things had not been spoiled—and now this!

Oh, Gail, she was thinking, if only you had not run away again. How can we find you?

Helen reached Doug by telephone. He was as upset as she, but she asked him to come over just the same. And Doug did.

The dinner was not what Helen had originally planned. Instead they ate a bite together at the kitchen table, though neither was very hungry.

"If only I knew where to find her," sighed Doug.

"I'm sure she will call. We are good friends. Friendship

should hold together in thick or thin. She should know that."

"She feels she has let us down, Helen. Gail has so much pride, but she should know that all we care about is her."

They sat in Helen's living room waiting for the phone to ring, but the hours ticked away and there was no call. Finally Doug went home to the parsonage, looking tired and dejected. He had not bothered to conceal what his heart felt. Helen could see in his eyes how much he cared.

After Doug had gone, she went into Gail's room. Everything was in order. There were still some of her clothes hanging in the closet. How much she would be missed!

Perhaps she will still call, Helen thought, but the evening passed and soon it was after midnight, with still no word.

15

It was all over. A thick fog seemed to cloud Barbara Omar's mind as she slowly tried to find her way out of the dimness and confusion. She realized she was lying in a bed in the recovery room, gradually coming out of the anesthetic. For a while Barbara was afraid to face reality, but finally she forced her hand to touch her left breast, and it was there—bandaged—but there! A joy that was almost heavenly swept through her whole being. All must be well. Then with a smile, she drifted back to sleep.

When Barbara next opened her eyes, she was back in her hospital room with Ernest sitting in the chair beside her bed. She smiled at him and he bent to kiss her.

"Welcome back, dear!" he said with a voice so jubilant that Barbara knew she had been right.

"You look happy!" she whispered.

"I'm the happiest guy in the world, Barb. All is well. You will be able to go home in a couple of days."

"The biopsy was negative, wasn't it, dear?"

"Yes, there was just a small cyst, completely benign, no sign of cancer. And those words, Barbara, are the most beautiful ones I can imagine. I feel as if suddenly life has been returned to me, because there would have been no living without you. I was worried and scared until I knew, and for the first time, even *I* had begun to wonder if there really was a curse over Golden Acre."

"We have licked that curse now." Barbara's voice was strong and confident. "From now on, everything will be fine. God is on our side. And soon we will find Gail! I just feel in my heart that from now on nothing can harm us."

Ernest took his wife's hand and patted it gently.

"And I have learned a great lesson. God is there when we call on Him, and He hears our mortal prayers. Barbara, I saw how helpless I was by myself. I may be a doctor and I can cut and scrape and mend, but only God can do the healing."

"How Mother would love to hear you say those words, Ern. She had such great faith in God and trusted Him in everything. She brought me up to believe that life was beautiful as long as God was our guide. But as I grew older and moved away from home, I lost much of that wonderful trust in God I once had. But I am finding it again now with great thankfulness, and I shall hold onto it. It's like finding a precious jewel that has been lost."

"And now you must rest, dear," ordered Dr. Omar. "No matter how good you feel, you have gone through surgery and you need a lot of rest. Soon we can return to our Golden Acre, and then I don't think it will be too long before we will be moved back into our Lexington house for the winter and I will return to my practice, busier and more dedicated than ever, I suppose."

"It all sounds so good, especially since we will not be losing our Golden Acre. It was there we learned the secret of life—that God is the key to happiness. And the house will be waiting and ready for us when we need its solitude and we can look forward to many glorious summers there."

"We won't lose a thing, Barb, not a thing. Life will be beautiful once more, and as soon as our girl comes back and the three of us are together again, we should never complain again."

Ernest Omar kissed his wife and tucked the blanket around her shoulders. She gave him a loving smile as he walked out of the room and closed the door softly behind him.

He is happy here, thought Barbara. This is his real world. Right now he must be walking up and down the corridors, mingling with the staff, inhaling the pungent odors characteristic of the hospital. And he would love every minute of it! She knew how anxious he was to get back to work, dressed in his white coat, visiting patient after patient in the rooms around her, smiling and encouraging them, and once again feeling himself whole again, using his talent, exercising his art of healing. Thank God that he was sure of himself once more.

Golden Acre had been a strange experience for them. Loving it as they did, they had now completed their plans of fixing it up. It was a special plot of land nestled beneath the high mountain, really belonging to them alone. The house, standing there with its coat of yellow paint, white ruffly curtains in the window, was embraced by thick growths of spruce, pine, oak, and maple, with an occasional white flash of birch. In the summer the emerald lawn stretched out for almost an acre—that sought-after acre of peace. They had furnished the house to their liking and from within could see the lake with the loons giving their eerie call as dusk fell over all nature. Ernest

had his boat in which he could spend time fishing and
Barbara had her wishing well. Yes, they loved it all and
were grateful for its comfort.

All would be perfect if only Gail returned home soon.
Barbara's mother-heart would never stop aching until she
knew that her child was safe and secure, and she could
see and talk with her again. Where could Gail be? All this
time had passed with no sign of her whereabouts. But
Barbara refused to give up hope. She tried to assure herself that all would end happily, but just now her heart
refused to confirm her thoughts.

Presently Barbara's thoughts encompassed all the
mothers whose hearts were aching because their children
had wandered away from the love and security of home
and parents. She had read in newspapers, from time to
time, of similar cases, but then they had seemed so remote. Now she understood the pain of separation and the
helplessness and anxiety of waiting day after day for a
sign or a word.

The world was full of danger. Barbara had been blessed
to come through her ordeal and was now assured of her
own health, but this hospital was filled with people who
were approaching the end and who tried to remain stoic
and courageous. She was glad that Ernest was going to
dedicate his life anew to helping mankind. She was proud
of him and glad to be his wife and prayed that God would
guide his skilled hands.

There would be a new change of direction for all of
them. Golden Acre had not been a mistake. It would be
there as a haven when they most needed it. Their error
had been in running away: she from the oft-frantic rush of
the city, Ernest from the frustrations of his demanding
profession, and Gail, like a pouting child, from the disappointment of interrupted plans. They had *all* acted like

children and forgotten the strength which comes from faith in the Father. Surely this power would lead them back. How had Gail put it? *This was the only world they had.* Barbara Omar drifted off to sleep. It was a sound, healing sleep—strength would soon return and life begin anew.

When Ernest came to the hospital that night he sensed that she had taken a great stride in the right direction. Dr. Haas had also visited, telling her how pleased he was with the operation and that she could go home in two days. And Lois had come to keep her company while their doctor-husbands talked business in another part of the hospital.

"You look great," said Lois Haas. "We are both so thrilled with the results."

They talked until the men returned.

Barbara's room was filled with flowers. Her favorites were Ernest's two dozen long-stemmed red roses, whose fragrant beauty she would enjoy for these two days of rest. And soon she could get up and walk around—and the days would pass quickly and then she would go home again—which was the most wonderful thought of all.

Barbara called Mrs. Briggs on the phone and gave her the happy news.

"You see," she said, "there is no curse at Golden Acre. You can just forget about that now."

"I will," promised Mrs. Briggs. "I promise that after Gail comes back, I shall never speak of it again."

"How is Lady?"

"Oh, that dog is a wonder. We have fallen in love with her. My husband and I have decided to get a dog too. We never realized what company a pet could be."

"I know a dog will give you a lot of pleasure, and then Lady will have a pal to play with."

"Well, I am so glad for you, and Lady will be glad, too. See you soon. It will be good to have you home again."

After Barbara had hung up the phone, she began to think of what fine friends the Briggses had become. They had gone through sorrow, deep personal loss, but they had raised themselves above their troubles. They had gained understanding and in return, given comfort to others in pain and suffering.

That night as Ernest sat beside her, they talked about the future and the mistakes of the past.

"You know, Barb," he said, "it is strange to realize that if we only follow the right path, we will find happiness."

"I know, Ern, in spite of the pain, this last year has been good for us. We have grown in wisdom and in love both for our family and for the world."

When Barbara went to sleep that night, she knew that in only two more days this time of her life would have passed. The tears and fears would be forgotten and she would be stronger in body and in soul. And Barbara knew that her talent must be used in being a helpmate to the man she loved and making their home dearer than any other place on earth.

16

The whole thing was unreal! It didn't seem possible that it could have happened. Could it have been just this morning that she had opened her eyes in her bedroom in Earthend and smiled at the whole world because everything was so wonderful? The sunshine had poured in through the window and the mountains outside had a bluish tint. She was no longer worried about Linda Butler's presence in town because from the way Doug had talked to her over the phone the afternoon before, she knew without a doubt that he loved her and could not wait to come back to hold her in his arms.

Helen had remarked about how happy she looked.

"You must know something you haven't told me," she had teased at the breakfast table. "Your eyes are sparkling like stars."

"Well, that's because Doug is coming home today! I know I am in love, but *you* have known that for a long time."

Helen laughed merrily so that her whole body shook.

169

"My mother used to say that when the love bug bites, he certainly leaves a mark. And I know you have been bitten."

They always had such a companionable time together and Helen had asked Gail her plans for the day. Gail had told her and then they had parted. But never would Gail have dreamt that when the day was over, everything in Earthend would be finished for her and that she would be far away from the town and the two people who meant so much to her. Now here she was, sitting in a hotel room in Pittsburgh, thinking back over the day.

Gail had been too happy to work when she arrived at the church office. There wasn't much to do anyway. She took out the list of sick people that Doug was supposed to have called on when he returned and placed a telephone call to each family, telling them that their pastor would be home late that day and that he would see them as soon as he could arrange it. She had meant to make some visits for him, but she knew she couldn't concentrate!

Then all at once, she covered her typewriter and straightened out the office.

"I'm taking the day off just to be happy," she had told herself. "I'm going home and fix myself up so I'll look especially pretty and then I'll just relax and wait for Doug. After all, he's the one who told me to take time off whenever I felt like it. And this is the day."

Gail had walked briskly the short distance to Helen Armstrong's house. There she saw the little red flag on the back door, a signal that Helen left when she was going to be away for a while. Gail was in the best of spirits when she unlocked the door and entered the kitchen. It always made her feel warm and cozy to come into the house.

Then she saw the newspaper spread out on the kitchen table, and there was her own face looking up at her.

Hastily she read the impersonal black print and then her whole world tumbled. She wondered where Helen had gotten the paper and why her dad had contacted the police and detectives to try to find her. She knew that her folks would be worried but had never thought they would take such drastic measures. But of course they'd try anything to find her! Never had she doubted their love for her, even as their plans had so distressed her.

For a moment she was lost. She didn't know just what to do, except that she could not stay here and cause embarrassment to Doug who had so carefully planted her in Earthend. This might cause a scandal: he had picked up a runaway and let her work with him. And Helen—dear warm, generous Helen—what would she think of the young girl to whom she had given so much friendship and happiness? She must go quickly, as she couldn't bear to face them now. She would have to leave a note. Perhaps Helen's bedroom would be the best place to leave it. Helen might not go there right away and that would give Gail a little time before she found it.

Gail dashed off a message and packed a few things in her tote bag, leaving the rest. She couldn't carry too much on her flight, not really knowing how she would get out of town. But she must hurry, before Helen arrived home. Gail could not bear to see Helen or the hurt look in her eyes.

Thinking back now, Gail was grateful that she had gotten a ride so easily. She had felt miserable when she closed the door to Helen's house. All the happiness was gone from her heart, leaving it anxious and bewildered. Outside, the sunshine was gone and the day had turned bleak and cold, but she started out bravely, taking the road that led to the highway. As she rounded the gas station on the corner, she spotted a large produce truck, the driver ready to get in. He was a middle-aged man with a friendly face and work-worn hands. She thought she had seen him in town on a few occasions.

Gail walked up to him bravely.

"Are you headed for Pittsburgh?" she asked.

"I guess that's the only way to head," he laughed.

"Would you consider giving me a lift out of town? I have to catch a plane and there isn't even a bus going out of here."

He studied her for a moment.

"How do you usually get out of town?" he asked.

"The preacher always drives me, but he is away on an emergency and I have to get away today, so I thought of hitchhiking."

"A young girl like you should be more careful," he warned.

"I looked you over very carefully before I asked," Gail smiled.

The gas station owner, who had been listening to the whole conversation, assured the truck driver:

"She's all right, Charlie. This is Gail Olsen, the pastor's secretary, at that little white church over there."

"Okay! That's good enough for me," said Charlie. "Hop in."

Gail rode in the truck for a couple of hours and then took a bus the rest of the way to Pittsburgh. There she found a family-type hotel and checked in, and now she was alone in a room, her heart aching with longing for the little town she had just left.

Gail had done a lot of thinking today. She had gone over her life in detail since that August morning when she had left Golden Acre. Now she realized that she must go back to New Hampshire and face the consequences that might be awaiting her there and try to make a fresh start. The only thing she really wanted was Doug, and she was sure that she had lost him. She would not be the kind of wife he was looking for, he with his high principles and strong character. She would try not to think about him—how she would manage to do that she did not know—but she just knew that she had to. I have grown up these months I have been away, she was thinking. I have learned a great deal about the real values of life. Doug taught me so much and now I will try to act like an adult instead of a child.

That evening Gail had stood in front of the telephone many times, but she could not make herself call her folks' number. She had called the airport, though, and made a reservation on a plane for Boston the following morning.

Finally her fingers touched the phone and she dialed the number and heard the ringing at the other end, but there was no answer. A little later, she tried again, but there was still no answer. Her parents must be away.

Gail paced the floor restlessly. There was only one other way and that was to call the Briggses; they were always home and Mrs. Briggs was such a dear, understanding person. Gail still remembered the number to the house on the mountaintop, but her hands trembled as she dialed. In a few seconds she heard Mrs. Briggs's voice. Gail choked up at the sound and could not answer right away. Mrs. Briggs repeated her *hello* several times.

Finally Gail spoke.

"Mrs. Briggs . . . this is me . . . Gail."

For a moment there was silence. Then . . . .

"Oh, Gail, my dear! Is it really you? I'm so glad to hear your voice. Where have you been? We have all been frantic with worry; there's been no trace of you."

"I guess I did something very foolish. I'm sorry—so

sorry. But where are Mom and Dad? I have called and called, but there's no answer."

"Your mom is in the hospital. She had an operation, but she will be home the day after tomorrow. Where are you calling from?"

"I'm in a hotel in Pittsburgh, Pennsylvania, right now, on my way home. I have a ticket on a flight to Boston tomorrow morning."

"Come right along! Mr. Briggs and I will fetch you at the airport."

"But it's too far for you to drive to Boston."

"Nonsense! What time shall we meet you?"

"I am coming in at 2:00 P.M. But please, tell me what is the matter with Mom?"

"It was nothing serious. She's fine now. We'll fill you in on the details when we see you, and Gail, you'd better stay with us until your folks come home."

"Thanks a million, Mrs. Briggs. It will be good to talk to you."

"We are so happy that you are safe. Please, Gail, be there when we get to the airport tomorrow."

"I'll be there, I promise. See you then."

It felt good to talk to Mrs. Briggs. Gail was touched that she seemed so glad to hear from her. She even managed to get to sleep without tears.

Gail's flight the next day was a smooth one and arrived right on time. When she entered the terminal, there were her two neighbors waiting for her.

There was so much to talk about on the ride home. Gail told the Briggses about her experiences in the little town of Earthend, although she didn't mention that she was in love with the preacher.

It was a bittersweet experience for Gail to drive past

Golden Acre and up the familiar steep hill to the Briggses' house. When they arrived, Gail met Lady for the first time. Lady sniffed and looked her over for a few minutes and finally licked Gail's hand.

"I'm so glad she's our dog," she said, stroking Lady's soft coat. "I know we'll be friends."

Gail slept well that night, in spite of the thoughts of Earthend which crowded her mind. Now the excitement of seeing Mom and Dad again must take precedence.

The next day, the Briggses drove her down to the Omars' house and Lady stayed with her willingly. What a surprise it would be when her parents came home and found her there!

What a beautiful home we have, Gail thought, as she went from room to room looking at everything. Now she would love and appreciate it and try to live the way Doug had taught her. Could she not serve others without hurting her family? She would try.

It was early afternoon when her parents' car drove up the driveway. Lady began to bark and wag her tail; she ran to the door to wait. Gail, too, started for the door, but stood frozen in the emotions of the reunion. When her father unlocked it, she was standing in the middle of the foyer, smiling through her tears. Dr. Omar gently guided Barbara through the open doorway and Gail was in her mother's arms, and then in her dad's. Not many words were spoken at first—it was a time for hugs and tears of thanksgiving.

"This is the nicest homecoming I could ever have had," said Barbara Omar.

"And I am so happy to be back. Can you ever forgive me?"

"There is nothing to forgive, dear. We were wrong to

try to shut you away from life. We are so grateful to have you here—now we can all have a second chance."

"Your mom has to go to bed now, after the long drive," said Ernest. "She is still not very strong, but she is very lucky. Come up to our bedroom and we will fill you in on everything that has happened to us."

There was much talking that day and long into the night.

Gail told them about Earthend, about Helen and Doug, about the church, and then about the newspaper article and her speedy departure.

"I was ready to tell Doug everything if I had only had a little more time. And I wanted so to call you, but I was ashamed and a little scared, I think."

"Well, that's all over now, and we shall have to get in touch with this young preacher of yours and thank him for taking care of you."

"Let's wait just a little longer. I still don't think I could talk to him without crying."

"We will wait as long as you want us to, dear. Don't worry. We can always write to him, you know."

And as the days went by, Gail took over the household duties to make the time go by more quickly. Sunday came and Gail's mind followed the church service in Earthend. How clearly she could see Doug standing there in his black robe preaching the Word of God, straight from his heart. She knew he would miss seeing her in her regular pew, but perhaps Linda Butler was sitting there now, starry-eyed, glad that Doug's secretary was nowhere in sight. Gail wondered if they all knew about her or if Helen and Doug had kept her identity to themselves. She searched for the courage to go back to Earthend. Never had she wanted anything more in her whole life than to be back with Doug in Helen's old house in that remote mountain town.

One day her dad brought up the subject of Skidmore.

"We could try for the spring semester," he said. "We'll do all we can to get you in."

"Thanks, Dad," said Gail. "I am not really so set on going now, as I once was. Perhaps I will just let it go this year and try to find myself."

Ernest looked lovingly at his pretty daughter.

"And perhaps you will find your preacher again? That is what you really want, isn't it?"

"More than anything, Dad. I'd like to marry Doug and move to that little town and help him with his work."

"I think it's time to get in touch with him," Dr. Omar smiled. "I'd like to meet him."

"I don't think so. I know Doug. If he wants me, he will find me. But I'm not very sure that he will. I think I'd like to leave it that way."

Gail had tried to set her life straight. She had talked to Fran several times over the phone and had called Lynn in California. They were both glad to talk to her and relieved that she was home. Neither girl asked too many questions. Perhaps they knew that when she was ready, she would share with them the happenings of the two and a half months she had been away.

Barbara was getting stronger each day and still beaming over her good fortune at having escaped the malignancy of cancer. Soon it was time to get things at Golden Acre ready for closing it for the winter. The Haases were moving out of the Lexington house in a couple of weeks and the Omars would be returning to their old house for the winter months. Ernest was anxious to get back to his office and to the hospital. It had been such a good feeling to visit there during Barbara's illness. Now to get back full-time would be a real challenge.

One afternoon, when Gail had been home a little over a week, she sat reading in the living room. Lady was sleeping at her feet and her mother, her strength returning, was poking around in the kitchen. Her dad was in the basement putting away his fishing tackle until next season. When Barbara came into the living room to join her daughter, Gail put down her book.

"It is so good to have you home, dear," Barbara said —words that she must have repeated a hundred times since Gail's return.

"And it is good to be home, Mom. I think we all have found ourselves. In a way, we are a better, stronger family for what has happened."

"Yes, your dad said that the other night. And he has truly found his Golden Acre. Every soul on earth, I think, must search for one, but he had it right in his hands and didn't even know it. Now we know that to fulfill our task on earth is to do our best in whatever talent God has given us. That is our very own Golden Acre. It isn't a place. It's an experience, a challenge, a sacred duty, whatever you may call it. Dad knows that to be a surgeon is a very special calling and now he thanks God for his knowledge and skill. I'm sure that whenever he operates there will be a prayer in his heart that a higher, stronger hand will guide his hands."

"I think that is wonderful," smiled Gail. "And perhaps it is worth all we went through to find that."

The doorbell chimed.

"I'll get it," called Dr. Omar, coming up the cellar stairs.

Lady barked and started for the door, but Gail patted her and held her back.

"It's all right, Lady. It's probably just the Briggses and you love having company."

There were voices speaking in muted tones in the foyer and then Dr. Omar appeared in the living room with the two callers. Gail found herself staring at two very precious faces. Right beside her dad, in the familiar brown leather jacket, stood Douglas Rhodes, and beside him was dear, smiling Helen Armstrong.

Gail rose to her feet. She opened her mouth to speak, but no words came. She wanted to throw herself in their arms, but her feet did not move. When she finally did speak, her words seemed wooden and stilted.

"I'm so very glad to see you both! Welcome to Golden Acre. I was hoping you would come looking for me. This is my mom, Mrs. Omar, and you have already met my dad."

A tear rolled down Helen's cheek.

"We waited and waited to hear from you, Gail. I was sure you would come to your senses and call me. How could you run off like that? Didn't you know how dear you are to us?"

Then Gail flew into Helen's arms and felt them holding her tightly as though Helen would never let her go. Gail reached out and took Doug's hand, awkward in the silence of his steady gaze.

"Oh, you will never know how much I wanted to get in touch with both of you. But I thought I had hurt you so much and messed up your lives. I really didn't know how you felt about Gail *Omar*. But I am so grateful that you came. I can never thank you enough."

"We found your address in the paper and we wanted to

be sure that you were here," continued Helen. "We couldn't rest easy until we knew that you were safely home. That's where the church people in Earthend think you have gone for a visit. We are the only two who know your story and we will keep it that way."

"Thanks," said Gail. "I'm so happy that you found me. Of course you'll stay for the night."

"Yes," said Barbara, "do stay with us for a while."

"I'm on my way to my grandmother's in Vermont," Doug finally spoke, "but Helen can stay here until I come back."

"Can I come?" asked Gail. "Once you said I could meet her."

"I'd be glad to have you ride with me if your folks agree." (Why was he so solemnly polite?—Gail wondered.)

"Gail is a big girl now," laughed Dr. Omar. "She can decide for herself."

"But we must have some coffee before you go," insisted Barbara.

It was only when they were seated in Doug's little sports car that they were finally alone. Doug started the motor and drove down the road without a word. Then he stopped the car with an uncharacteristic abruptness.

"You silly little fool," he said, sweeping her into his arms. "How could you do this to me? You knew that I loved you. And a secretary should not leave her job without permission."

"Are you going to fire me?" whispered Gail, snuggling deeper into his arms.

"Yes, that's why I came—to tell you that you are no longer needed in the church office. But how about coming to work for me in the parsonage?"

"That depends on my salary," teased Gail with such

happiness flooding her heart that she thought it was going to burst.

Doug kissed her tenderly.

"How soon can you come back, my dear?"

"After we have seen *our* Grandmother Rhodes, we'll talk it over with my parents. You see what an obedient gal I have become. But Doug, are you sure that you want me in spite of everything?"

Doug started up the car again.

"In spite of everything, dear, you are the only one I want in that big parsonage."

There was no need for more words, and Gail knew that right then and there she had found the meaning of life and a happiness so great that it would last forever.

17

On Christmas Eve there was going to be a wedding in the Community Church in Earthend, and it was the talk of the town. How to seat all the people who wanted to attend would be a problem, for the church was not that large. An invitation had been extended from the pulpit one Sunday morning, and an open notice had been printed in the town's paper, welcoming the whole town to the ceremony.

Pastor Douglas Rhodes was to marry Miss Gail Omar. Her name had been Olsen when she had first come to Earthend as the pastor's secretary, but then one day it had been corrected to Omar and no one knew just why. There was a rumor that she had called herself by her mother's maiden name because she had been so fond of her Norwegian grandmother. And even if it seemed a strange thing to do, the townspeople were not bothered. After all, what difference did it make when her name would be changed anyway, when she married their pastor? The whole story was like a fairy tale. The girl who had lived among them—baby-sitting, dusting and cleaning their houses, working with the sick, and helping wherever she was needed—was really the daughter of a wealthy, prominent surgeon from Boston. When it came to money, there seemed to be no lack of it. The family had invited the whole town to the reception—a Norwegian smorgasbord—in the Town Hall, soon to be decorated with wedding bells and flowers, and tables loaded with food, provided by a caterer from Boston.

No wonder people were excited! Nothing like this had ever happened in their town. And some of them were to be a part of the wedding. Mr. Morrison, the church moderator, and his wife were to be the official host and hostess. And the church choir was going to sing "O Promise Me" accompanied by their own organist. And goodhearted, plump Helen Armstrong had been chosen to be the matron of honor. It was so like Gail to do a thing like that, proving the love in her heart for the people of her adopted hometown. And Helen was having her gown made by a seamstress in Pittsburgh—an ankle-length dress of moss-green velvet with shoes dyed to match.

Two friends of Gail's were coming from quite a distance to be her bridesmaids—a girl named Fran from Lexington, Massachusetts, and Lynn, coming all the way from California. The minister who was to perform the ceremony had been a classmate of Doug's at the seminary and his best man was a childhood friend from Vermont. What a wedding it would be! There were only a few out-of-town guests: the bride's parents, the grandmother of the groom, some neighbors from New Hampshire named Briggs, and Dr. and Mrs. Haas from Lexington. None of them would have to worry about finding a motel room, for the church members were vying for the honor of entertaining the guests in their homes.

The church was to be decorated with red and white poinsettias, evergreen boughs, and holly-festooned candelabra, and the ceremony was to be at twelve noon—an unusual time for a wedding in Earthend.

The church board had requested the privilege of having a dinner for the bridal party and their out-of-town guests the night before the wedding, following the rehearsal. Now the basement social hall had been given a new coat of paint and had been decorated with wedding bells combined with pine branches and scarlet ribbons, until it looked like a real banquet room. The Ladies' Guild planned to serve a dinner of prime ribs of beef, stuffed baked potatoes, corn pudding, Pennsylvania Dutch relishes, fruit salad, and a dessert of decorated ice creams. Meanwhile, Mr. Mason, the local baker, was outdoing himself preparing the cake for the reception!

The twenty-third of December arrived with bright sunshine glistening on a light powder of white snow which had fallen during the night, covering the dirt-trodden drifts left from the last snowstorm. It was as if even nature was cooperating to make this the most beautiful setting possible for a winter wedding.

And all went according to schedule. The arriving guests received a warm welcome from the prospective bride and groom, and finally the family arrived, to many hugs and kisses. The rehearsal and banquet went off without a flaw and soon the darkness of night had crept over the mountain and settled over the town. When dawn arrived, Christmas Eve was as lovely a day as the one before, and long before the appointed hour the church was filled to the last pew. Sunshine poured in through the stained-glass windows, filling the church with glorious color, but not quite reaching to the altar where stately white candles softly and gently cast their warm glow.

The organist played traditional wedding music especially selected to set an atmosphere of reverence and expectant joy. The groom's grandmother was ushered slowly up the aisle in a dress of soft gold trimmed with bright green. Her corsage was of tiny red rosebuds and lily of the valley. She looked fragile and delicate but her dainty head, framed in silvery-white hair, was proudly erect. Everyone in town knew that she had just recovered from a serious illness and they were pleased that she could be there. A hush fell, as the choir sang of love's promise and abiding power.

Then, the mother of the bride, looking young and lovely in a shimmering blue gown with red velvet sash and an identical corsage, was ushered to her seat. All was ready—and the organist struck the first chords of the Wedding March and the congregation rose in anticipation. The groom and his best man came in from a side door and the ushers unrolled the white carpet. As the music soared, the two bridesmaids, side by side, moved slowly up the aisle in their red velvet gowns. Their chestnut curls were crowned by garlands which matched their bouquets of carnations and white mums. Next came Helen Armstrong, a contrast in muted green, carrying yellow carnations and mums. Finally appeared Gail, the girl all Earthend had learned to love and admire, a vision in white tulle and lace, floating up the aisle like a cloud on her handsome father's arm. She seemed unaware of the congregation; her eyes looked only to her groom, waiting by the altar. His eyes were glowing with happiness as he beheld his beautiful bride coming closer and closer until she stood beside him and the last chord faded into silence.

So they stood there—the two lovers—counting the

moments until the miracle of words would bind them together for all time and eternity with the blessing of God's love.

The wedding was breathtakingly beautiful. It was joyous, sacred, and touching. Each person sitting in his pew felt the impact of a love that made it possible for humans to find a piece of heaven amid the turmoil of this world. The ceremony was brief, but there were some people seen to wipe away a tear as the newlyweds walked past, wreathed in joyful smiles—now one in all things.

The reception was even more spectacular than the guests had anticipated. The bride and groom took time to talk and receive good wishes from each guest. Doug and Gail stood in the receiving line for a long, long time, but their smiles never faded and their handshakes remained firm and warm. The townspeople showered the couple with good wishes, not just for the present, but for a lifetime. After all, Gail and Doug belonged to this little town with its plain, hardworking people and to this church which diligently labored to plant God's peace in every heart.

What a gay party the reception was—with Christmas carols and candlelight and laughter and gentle togetherness at this holy season. And the food! Well, Earthend had never seen anything like it. Not only did it taste superb, but its magnificent quantity might even have outdone the Scandinavian countries. Long before the reception had ended, the bridal couple slipped away unnoticed. They left the hall and quickly sped off on the highway that Christmas Eve afternoon, the driver with his arm around his bride.

"It was a beautiful wedding, Doug," whispered Gail, her heart beating fast with happiness.

"The most beautiful in the world," said Doug, giving Gail an extra squeeze.

"Doug, I am so happy."

"I hope that will last forever and ever, dearest."

And Doug stopped the car right in the middle of the deserted highway and gave his wife a proper kiss, for they had a long drive ahead and he could not wait any longer to perform this pleasant duty of a husband. Then they started off for Pittsburgh where they would spend their wedding night before flying to Florida to stay in a guest cottage in West Palm Beach, an extra wedding gift from Dr. Omar. They would only be away a week, but they planned to fill that week with happiness, togetherness, and fun.

They drove in silence for a while. There was no need for words. Just as they had been united in marriage before God by the minister, so now they knew that their souls had also been wed, so completely did they belong to each other.

Gail was thinking back over the last few months, the agony and struggle she had suffered. She had felt torn apart—one part of her rebelling against her parents; the other part wanting to trust and love them as she always had. She had followed wrong instincts. Too late had she understood that her mom and dad only wanted the best for her. Then there had been the fight within her—a conflict that so often besets the young—the fight to be free.

Gail closed her eyes to dream a little. Her grabbed-for freedom had brought her to Doug and she knew she must have loved him at once. If only she had been honest with him from the start, how much heartache could have been avoided. But God had taken things into His own hands, and He had given her more than she deserved: her heart's sincere desire—to work with Doug in his little church. Grandmother Olsen would have been glad for her. She would have loved Doug, too. Gail knew that she was very much like her grandmother and those precious seeds that Grandmother Olsen had planted in her granddaughter's heart had borne fruit for God's Kingdom. Gail had been such a little girl when Grandmother had told her of the wonders and majesty of God and she had wanted then to serve Him with all her heart. Perhaps that was to be her *Golden Acre*. But after Grandmother had died, Gail had slipped away from those teachings for a while. Now she had rediscovered them and they would stay in her heart forever. She would serve God always, working beside her preacher-husband wherever God directed them. Gail's heart bubbled over with joy—now she knew her goal.

Presently Doug slowed the car as if he were looking for something. They must have traveled many miles, Gail was thinking.

"Are you asleep, Gail?" he asked softly.

"O no, Doug, I have never been more awake. I feel as if I am just beginning to live. But I have been thinking back over the last few months since we have known each other, wondering how I ever lived before I met you. I can't even remember what life was like then. And to think, now I belong to you forever and ever."

"Yes, dearest, forever and ever!" Doug drew her close to him. "You are my gift from God, my Christmas gift at that, the most wonderful gift I've ever had."

Gail smiled.

"And God gives such good gifts! Didn't He give the best gift to the world that first Christmas when He gave His Son to the world, to save us all. How much He must have loved this world! Christmas is love!"

"God is love," corrected Doug, "and now you and I can

give His gift to so many. What a team we will make together. But here we are, Gail."

Doug slowed the car to a stop by the side of the road.

"I'd like to stop here for a few minutes. I don't know if you recognize this spot in winter, but this is our lake. This is where I first confessed my love for you. I'd like to go down that path again now, when the girl I fell in love with is my wife."

"Oh, I know where we are," said Gail. "I was so deep in thought I didn't recognize it at first. It's nice to be back even if there are no ducks to feed."

Hand in hand they walked down to the lake, now a frozen sheet of ice. Beside the lake stood the trees, bare and lonely, except for a few pines and spruces that were always green, making it look less deserted.

"You know," said Gail, half in jest, "if we were living in Old Testament days, we would build an altar to the Lord, right on this spot. Isn't that what God's people did when something wonderful happened to them? Too bad we aren't living way back then."

"We don't have to be living in biblical times to build a shrine to our God, Gail. We can do it right now. That stone by the lake can be our altar. Come, let's kneel there together."

It was a sacred moment for the newlyweds as Doug and Gail knelt in the snow by the stone. Doug held Gail's hand as he prayed in his deep voice.

Great Lord God, Gail and I have come to this altar to dedicate ourselves to Your service. We dedicate our lives to serve You and humanity, and to do all we can to see that Your will is done here on earth as it is in heaven. Bless our marriage and help us to be worthy of each other. Together we praise Your holy name. Amen.

As they rose from their knees, it seemed to Gail that Doug's *Amen* still lingered on the air like the sound of a bell echoing through the universe, filling both earth and sky, a new song carried by the wind far and wide.

In silence they walked back to the car and started off again; words might have broken the spell they were under. It was not a spell, but the presence of God in a new dimension that Gail had never before experienced.

Then she realized that something had taken place in her soul—a transformation, a holy reverence, a rebirth that she knew would change her life from now on. And the melody of Doug's prayer began anew, jubilant and strong within her joyful heart . . . So be it . . . So be it. She had found her *Golden Acre* and never again would she fail to meet life in its fullness. Never again would she run away from its challenge, for she had found the truth and the truth had set her free.